She was out of control…

Lily pushed Brian back into the leather seat of the limo. Brushing his shirt aside, she smoothed her hands over his chest, hard and muscular, then leaned forward and pressed her lips to the soft dusting of hair beneath his collarbone. But when she let her fingers drop to his trousers, Brian grabbed her hands and drew them away.

"Are you sure about this, Lily?"

She smiled. He didn't have to be such a gentleman, but Lily was glad he made the attempt. "There's nothing wrong with two…" She moved back to his trousers. "Consenting adults…" She worked the button open. "Engaging in mutually satisfying…" She slowly drew the zipper down. "Sex."

Most guys had probably dreamed about hearing those words. And Lily never dreamed she'd be the one saying them. But she'd had enough of "relationships." What was wrong with taking her pleasure where she found it?

"Haven't you ever just been swept away by the moment?" she asked, playfully nipping at his neck.

"Yeah," Brian groaned, pulling her closer to him. "I think that's happening now…."

Dear Reader,

It's hard to believe that I'm almost at the end of my
Quinn saga. Yet another handsome Quinn brother has
fallen victim to love, and this time I almost didn't want
to type the last page of the manuscript. I've gotten used
to having these Quinns around!

Conor, Dylan, Brendan, Keely and Liam all found
love, and now it's Brian's turn. And this stubborn
and single-minded news reporter needed just the right
kind of woman to tempt him. Public relations expert
Lily Gallagher was the one, though falling in love was
the last thing she wanted to do.

I've been so grateful for all the notes that you've sent
me about the Quinns and I hope you'll follow their
stories right to the end. Next month Brian's twin
brother, Sean, meets his match. And after that, I guess
I'm going to go through a little Quinn withdrawal. But
I'm sure I'll find a handsome hero waiting around the
next corner.

Be sure to visit my Web site at www.katehoffmann.com
for information on all my releases.

Happy reading,

Kate Hoffmann

Books by Kate Hoffmann

THE MIGHTY QUINNS miniseries
847—THE MIGHTY QUINNS: CONOR
851—THE MIGHTY QUINNS: DYLAN
855—THE MIGHTY QUINNS: BRENDAN
933—THE MIGHTY QUINNS: LIAM

Harlequin Single Title—REUNITED

Kate Hoffmann
THE MIGHTY QUINNS: BRIAN

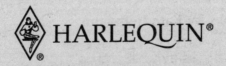

HARLEQUIN®

TORONTO • NEW YORK • LONDON
AMSTERDAM • PARIS • SYDNEY • HAMBURG
STOCKHOLM • ATHENS • TOKYO • MILAN • MADRID
PRAGUE • WARSAW • BUDAPEST • AUCKLAND

ISBN 0-373-69137-8

THE MIGHTY QUINNS: BRIAN

Copyright © 2003 by Peggy A. Hoffmann.

Visit us at www.eHarlequin.com

Printed in U.S.A.

Prologue

WIND-DRIVEN RAIN LASHED at the windows of the house on Kilgore Street. The storm had rolled off the North Atlantic a day ago, a nor'easter with the force of a tropical hurricane and the chill of a midwinter blizzard. Brian Quinn stared out at the flooded street from the second-story bedroom window, his forehead pressed against the glass.

He knew the *Mighty Quinn* was a seaworthy boat and that it had weathered storms much worse than this, but Brian still couldn't banish the worry from his head. Seamus Quinn was a great captain and he didn't need the Coast Guard to tell him the forecast—he felt it, he smelled it in the air and saw it in the clouds. But the *Mighty Quinn* was late coming in, already six days past the longest trip that Brian's father had ever made. And Brian could see the worry in Conor's eyes and the grim set of Dylan's mouth. They were worried, too.

The fishing had been bad all summer and the *Mighty Quinn* had been forced farther and farther out to find swordfish. But now, the season was winding down and the weather becoming more unpredictable. After the last trip, Conor had tried to convince their father to head south as so many other fishermen did during the fall and winter.

Though it would mean the six Quinn boys would be on their own for five or six months, Conor had assured

Seamus that he could handle things at home as long as the money kept coming in. He had run the household for seven years now, ever since their mother had walked out. Conor cooked and cleaned, he helped with homework and meted out discipline. And he tried his hardest to keep their situation from teachers and neighbors and anyone who might consider Seamus a neglectful father. A heavy load for a fourteen-year-old.

Brian glanced over his shoulder. His twin brother Sean was already in bed, the threadbare quilt pulled up around his chin, his nose buried in a comic book. Liam, the youngest Quinn, had crawled into bed next to Sean, curling up against him for warmth. The seven-year-old had given up begging his brother to read the comic for him and was now mouthing the words as he read for himself.

"Bri! Check those buckets in the hall," Dylan shouted from the bottom of the stairs. "It won't do any good if they overflow."

Brian sighed. One of these days there would be enough money to fix the leaky roof and to paint the sagging porch and to pay the phone bill before it got disconnected. There was always the next run to the Grand Banks and dreams of a hold full of swordfish and the chance to offload first and command the highest price. But Brian had learned that his father's big dreams very rarely came true.

Though they didn't talk about their father's drinking and gambling out loud, Brian knew his older brothers had tried their best to deal with the lack of money. Conor had taken to meeting the *Mighty Quinn* when it came in, hoping to deter Seamus from a visit to the pub and a drunken all-night poker game. And Dylan had learned to hide the money jar after Seamus got home, knowing that it would gradually disappear at their father's hand.

"He's not comin' home tonight," Sean said. "He won't bring the boat in in this weather."

"Is Da all right?" Liam asked.

"Yeah, he's all right," Brian murmured, getting up from the window. He wandered out to the hall and checked the row of buckets that Conor had set out to counter the leaking roof. Then he hurried back to the bedroom and hopped into bed, pulling the covers up over his chest.

If he just went to sleep, then it would be morning and the storm would be over and his father would be home and everything would be all right. "Your feet are cold, Li," Brian complained. "Keep 'em to yourself, ya little dosser."

"Shut yer gob," Liam said. "Read me. Come on, Sean. Read me just a little."

The stairs creaked. "Conor's coming up," Sean said. "Ask him for a story."

But instead of Conor, their brother Brendan poked his head in the room. "Con says lights out," he said. "School tomorrow."

"Will Da be home tomorrow?" Liam asked.

Brendan forced a smile then shrugged. "Don't know, Li. But he'll be home soon."

Liam sat up and brushed his hair out of his eyes. "Is he all right? My teacher said the storm was bad."

Brendan sat down on the edge of the bed and grabbed Liam's foot beneath the quilt, tickling it playfully. "Of course he'll be all right. Da can steer through any old storm." He glanced back and forth between Brian and Sean, a silent warning not to contradict him.

"Yeah," Brian agreed. "When I went out with Da last summer, he told me about a storm that had fifty-foot waves and wind so strong it could blow a man right off the deck. This isn't near as bad, Li."

Liam's expression shifted, now more worried. "How high are the waves?"

"They're just wee little waves," Brendan said. "Why don't you shove over and I'll tell you a story." He crawled in between Liam and Brian, leaning back against the headboard. "What story do you want to hear?"

The stories were a Quinn family tradition and when Seamus was home, he told a different tale nearly every night. They were wonderful stories of their legendary ancestors, the Mighty Quinns, those brave and clever men who vanquished evil. But when Seamus told the stories, the fables also featured scheming women. At first, Brian hadn't understood why the Quinns distrusted women so. But then he'd come to realize that the tales were laced with Seamus's own opinions about women—opinions based on their mother's desertion.

Her name was never spoken in the presence of their father but Conor talked about her every now and then. She had been beautiful, with long dark hair and pretty green eyes. And though Brian had been only three when she left, he remembered one thing—the red flowered apron that she wore every morning. He could still feel the starched fabric between his fingers.

"Odran and the giant," Sean said.

"Murchadh Quinn, the mighty seaman," Liam suggested.

"Eamon and the enchantress," Brian insisted. Though Brendan was only eleven, he told the tales the best. He wove stories full of excitement and vivid images, better than any action movie or comic book.

"I just remembered a story that Da told a long time ago when Con and Dylan and I were younger," Brendan said. "I don't think you've ever heard this one. It's about Riddoc Quinn who was the smartest of all our Quinn ancestors. In fact, Riddoc Quinn knew everything."

"No one can know everything," Brian said.

"Ah, but Riddoc did. For he was a very watchful lad. He didn't talk much, but saw a lot." Brendan pointed to his temple. "And he was also a great thinker. Like me. And a little like Liam, too."

"Get on with the story, gobdaw," Sean said.

Brendan cleared his throat. "Riddoc Quinn lived in a tiny village on the Irish seacoast in a small stone cottage perched on a craggy cliff. His parents were plain and simple folk who couldn't read or write, but Riddoc taught himself to do both. He read every book in the village and when there were none left, he visited nearby towns to borrow more. But that wasn't enough. Riddoc spoke with every person who passed through the village, asking of their travels, wanting to know about the rest of the world."

"Is this going to be one of those stories that we're supposed to learn something from?" Sean muttered. "Like study hard and stay in school?"

Brendan reached over Liam's head and gave Sean a cuff. "Shut up or I'll make you tell the story. And you're just about the worst storyteller in all of Southie."

"Keep going!" Liam cried.

"Riddoc and his family lived near a powerful sorcerer named Aodhfin and Aodhfin had two daughters named Maighdlin and Macha. Aodhfin spoiled his daughters, giving them anything they wished for, conjuring up pretty dresses and expensive gifts. The beautiful Maighdlin became very selfish and greedy. Her sister Macha was a plain and guileless girl and so it was as they grew older. Maighdlin demanded more and more of her father, putting on the airs of a princess while Macha concentrated on her studies, learning Latin and Greek and reading great books.

"As time passed, Aodhfin knew that he'd have to choose an heir to his magical powers. Though Maighdlin was grasping and unfeeling, Aodhfin knew she could become a powerful sorceress, maybe the most powerful in the land. But Macha was compassionate and generous, the type of person who would use her power for good.

"The old sorcerer was torn between his two daughters and spent many sleepless nights pondering his decision. He asked his friends to help him, but they were unable to make a choice for they were afraid that if they chose wrong, they might suffer later. As he was walking in the forest one day, Aodhfin came upon a peasant and decided to ask his advice. The peasant grinned and told him, 'You should ask Riddoc Quinn for he will know the answer. He knows everything.'"

"He would know," Liam said. "Riddoc Quinn was the smartest boy in Ireland."

"That he was. But he wasn't just book-smart. Riddoc understood others, their flaws and their strengths, for he had met many people in his quest for knowledge and understanding and had learned from each of them.

"And so Aodhfin sent for Riddoc Quinn and brought him to his home, a dark castle deep in the forest. The old sorcerer couldn't believe that this boy dressed in rags was the person he sought. 'I have heard you possess great knowledge,' the sorcerer said. Riddoc nodded. 'Then I will leave the decision to you,' said the sorcerer. 'You will choose between my two daughters and tell me which one will become a great sorceress. But first, you must tell me how you plan to decide.' Riddoc thought about this for a long moment. 'I will give them a test,' he said. 'I will ask them three questions which they must answer honestly.'"

Sean groaned. "Oh, no. Like a spelling test? This is a dumb story. I want the Odran story."

"It's the right way to decide," Brian countered. "It's the most fair."

"The day of the test approached," Brendan continued, "and the sorcerer grew worried that Riddoc was not the right person for the job. After all, he possessed no mystical powers—he was just an ordinary boy. Perhaps it would be better to use magic, a potion or a spell to make the decision clear. For the first test, Riddoc placed three items on a table in front of each of the daughters—a ruby, pearl and a simple stone polished smooth by the sea. He asked Maighdlin to choose the most beautiful stone. Of course Maighdlin chose the ruby for it was the most valuable. But when he asked Macha, she chose the stone from the sea."

"Macha is too dumb to be a sorceress," Sean said.

"The sorcerer thought so, too," Brendan continued. "How could Macha be a sorceress if she couldn't even recognize the value of a jewel? But Riddoc saw that Macha recognized the beauty in simple things. The next question was more difficult. Riddoc brought three men before the girls—a handsome knight, a wealthy shopkeeper and a monk. He gave Maighdlin a pouch of gold coins and asked her to give it to the man who needed it most. But Maighdlin was not about to be fooled. She gave a third to the knight for his protection, a third to the shopkeeper for a bolt of silk, and a third to the monk for his blessing. When Macha came into the room and was faced with the same choice, she held on to the bag of gold. 'I cannot give this bounty to any of these men for none of them need it. The knight is cared for by his liege and the shopkeeper makes his living from the goods he sells. And the monk has taken a vow of poverty. Where is the poor farmer whose crop has failed or the mother who has too many children to feed?'''

Brian nestled down in the bed, pulling the covers up to his chin. The wind still rattled the windows and water still dripped into a plastic bucket beside the bed. But as he listened to Brendan's story, he felt the real world fade away. He saw the sorcerer's castle in his mind, the deep forest. He saw Riddoc's tiny cottage near the sea. Though he'd been born in Ireland, he remembered nothing of that country. But he could feel it pulsing through his body now.

"The old sorcerer sighed. Macha was too tender-hearted to ever wield great power. But Riddoc knew that Macha was kind and generous and sympathetic to those less fortunate. There was one final question that Riddoc decided to give to the daughters. 'You may ask me one question,' he said. 'A question that you want answered more than any other.' They pondered their choices for a long time. 'Will I be the most powerful sorceress in Ireland?' Maighdlin asked. 'Will I ever find true love?' Macha asked. This proved what Riddoc already knew—Macha had a pure heart. He turned to the sorcerer. 'You must give Macha your power,' he said."

"This is so mushy," Sean said. "I s'pose now Riddoc is going to kiss her and they'll fall in love and get married."

"Not yet," Brendan said. "Because before the sorcerer died, Maighdlin took Macha deep into the forest and left her there, certain that she'd be devoured by wolves or starve to death."

"Did she die?" Sean asked.

"No. For Riddoc knew that Maighdlin would try something evil. He watched over Macha and followed the girls wherever they went. And he rescued Macha from the forest. He took her back to the castle and told the sorcerer of Maighdlin's evil deed. It was only then that the sorcerer knew the answer to his question. Now he could die peacefully. And so Macha became a sorceress. And Riddoc her most trusted advisor."

"And Maighdlin?" Brian asked.

"She became a toad. A slimy warty toad with a purple nose."

Brian laughed and Liam giggled. Sean just blinked in confusion. "She didn't try to turn Riddoc into a toad?"

Brendan shook his head. "No. He was too smart to let that happen." He cleared his throat and continued. "After a time, Macha and Riddoc married. And they had sons, who had sons, who had sons. But none of them needed magical powers for they inherited something more valuable from their father—a clever mind and a thirst for knowledge."

"Are you sure Riddoc didn't throw Macha over the cliff?" Sean asked. "Or maybe he took her back into the forest and chopped off her head? Da tells his stories different."

"This isn't Da's story, it's mine," Brendan said.

Brendan always told the *Mighty Quinn* tales differently, Brian mused. In his versions, the women weren't always the villains. "I liked this story just the way you told it."

Brendan nodded. "I did, too. And now you know that we're descended from kings and queens, knights and ladies, plain farmers and a powerful sorceress. It's time for you to get to sleep. It's late." He crawled off the bed and pulled the blankets up around the three brothers. As he walked to the door, Brendan flipped off the light.

The room went dark and Sean rolled over, tugging on the blankets. Liam flipped over and nestled up against Brian for warmth and security. Brian threw his arm over his head and stared up at the ceiling. Images of the story still swirled in his head. The tale of Riddoc Quinn appealed to him—the clever boy and the beautiful sorceress living in their forest castle.

"Do you think Da is all right?" Liam asked, his voice timid.

"Da is a Quinn. He's like Riddoc, he's clever," Brian murmured.

"I'm scared. What if he doesn't come back? They'll come and get us and take us away. We'll never see each other again." Liam's voice trembled and Brian could tell he was on the verge of tears.

"Conor would never let that happen," Brian said. He reached out and smoothed his hand over his little brother's hair. "We'll be together forever. Don't worry, Li."

The little boy sobbed softly and burrowed under the covers. Brian curled beneath the threadbare blankets and closed his eyes. But sleep refused to come. When the house grew silent, he slipped out of bed and grabbed his winter jacket from the floor, pulling it on to ward off the chill in the air. As he passed the other bedroom, he peeked inside to find his older brothers sprawled out on their beds.

The stairs creaked as he tiptoed down. When he reached the front parlor, he sat down in front of the portable television that Dylan had rescued from a junk pile in the alley. Brian flipped it on and the snowy picture illuminated the dark room. The antenna, draped with tinfoil, did little to bring the picture into focus. Brian could barely make out the weather forecaster standing in front of the map.

"This is Storm Central on WBTN-TV. Forecasters say the storm is worsening in the North Atlantic. The waves are battering the New England coast and causing many residents to head for higher ground. The barometer continues to fall, which means that we're still not over the worst of the storm. Marinas from Long Island to Maine have reported hundreds of boats ripped from moorings and destroyed. Many commercial fishing boats have also been damaged, a blow to those fishermen who have already had a bad summer season."

Brian leaned forward, trying to study the map, wondering where in the Atlantic his father was. He'd traced the route on the school atlas, but it had looked so simple then. He'd been on the boat before, far from the sight of land. Out there, everything looked the same.

"Meanwhile, the Coast Guard has had its hands full with distress calls from boaters and fishermen caught out on the Atlantic when the storm blew up. The fishing boat *Selma B.* out of Boston sank after taking on water, but the crew was airlifted off the deck to the safety of a Coast Guard helicopter. The *Willow* put into Gloucester a few hours ago after a search by Coast Guard cutters. Their radio had been knocked out."

A knot twisted in Brian's stomach and a wave of nausea washed over him. They all knew the dangers that faced a commercial fisherman. Brendan's teacher had once said that commercial fishing was the most dangerous occupation of all, more dangerous than driving a race car or flying an airplane. That knowledge had stuck with Brian over the years and now it seemed like a weight pressing down on him.

He stared at the man on the screen. If anything happened to the *Mighty Quinn*, the newscaster would know first. He'd know if the boat was sinking. He'd know whether Seamus was alive or dead. Like Riddoc Quinn, this man knew everything.

Brian pulled his knees up under his chin and shivered, refusing to allow himself the luxury of tears. "Someday, I'll be the first to know. And then I won't ever have to worry again."

1

THE NEWSROOM WAS a picture of controlled chaos as Brian Quinn strode through. Weekends were always a little crazy, the junior staff at WBTN-TV working with a skeleton crew. As he walked to his cubicle, Brian tugged on the starched collar of the pleated shirt, the fabric chafing his neck. He didn't wear a tux often, but when he did he found the experience wholly uncomfortable.

He caught his reflection as he walked by a plate glass window. The monkey suit did have an undeniable effect on the ladies, though. What was it about a black suit and a bow tie that made women swoon? A tux was no more unusual than a white T-shirt and faded jeans. Brian frowned. Women seemed to like that combination as well. That and plain old boxer shorts.

Too bad this wasn't a social occasion, he mused. At least then, maybe the starched shirt would have paid off in the end. Though there were bound to be more than a few beautiful women at the fund-raiser tonight, Brian was attending the party for business reasons. And he never mixed business with pleasure.

"Look at you."

He glanced to the left and saw Taneesha Gregory leaning over the wall of one of the cubicles, her smile wide, her dark eyes bright with humor. Taneesha was his favorite cameraman—or camera *goddess* as she pre-

ferred to call herself. Shameless and fearless, she often
had to muscle her way through a crowd of male news
photographers to get the best shot, shoving her camera
into a person's face to catch the nuances of their reaction to a question. When it came to a hard-hitting investigative piece, Taneesha was the person Brian
wanted to be there to get the shot.

"Don't even start," he warned, wagging his finger at
her.

"You da bomb," she said, laughing and clapping her
hands. She came around the cubicle, then reached up
and straightened his bow tie. "But I think a tux is a little over the top for a weekend anchor. I hear you're doing the eleven o'clock news tomorrow night."

"Yeah. But the tux isn't for that. I'm working on a
story."

"I hope you don't need me for this story. Because
you know I don't wear a—"

"Dress," Brian finished. "Yes. I know. The last time
you wore a dress was your wedding."

"That's right," she said, brushing a speck of lint off
his shoulder. "And I promised Ronald that I'd wear a
dress on our silver wedding anniversary. That's still
eleven years off."

"Don't worry," Brian assured her. "Tonight I'm just
checking out a lead. Richard Patterson, our sleazy
neighborhood real estate developer is hosting a fund-
raiser tonight. And I'm going to crash the party and get
a look at his guests."

Taneesha groaned. "Are you still on that story? If the
boss finds out you're chasing Patterson around town,
he'll have your head. Or have you forgotten just how

much money Patterson spends on advertising with this station?"

"He's got six fast-food restaurants and a car dealership which represent a fraction of his total business worth. And it's station policy that the sales department and the news department are independent of each other."

"That's what they say, but without advertising, WBTN wouldn't exist. And you'd be left shouting your stories from the top of Beacon Hill."

"I know there's a story here," Brian said in a serious tone. "I can feel it. I'm going to corner him and see what happens. Hell, what can he do? All those rich folks and him wanting to buy a place on the social ladder. I don't think he's going to haul off and hit me."

"Are you crazy? They'll toss you out of there so fast you'll—"

"Don't you think the public has a right to know? Three other developers spend seven years in court, trying to get approval on that property. Patterson buys it and he gets the zoning variance within weeks. He paid for that variance and I want to know how much it cost him and who got the money."

"Guys like that cover their tracks well."

"Shady real estate deals, backroom bargaining and a lot of money changing hands. Sooner or later, they're going to get lazy and make a mistake. Patterson's deals always seem to come too easily. My brother-in-law, Rafe Kendrick, is a developer and even he says that Patterson isn't legal."

"You realize that the guy who owns this television station is an old friend of Richard Patterson's? Maybe you should think about your career here?"

Brian laughed. "I've become the top investigative reporter in Boston in just over a year and I pull in the viewers. They're not going to fire me."

"But they may not offer your cocky ass the weekend anchor position. And you know the weekend anchor will be the one to replace Bill when he retires in two years."

The rumors had been swirling around the station since the last ratings period but Brian tried not to listen to them. "You think I want to sit in front of a camera and read news for the rest of my career?" he asked.

"Well, you certainly have the face for it," Taneesha said, giving his cheek a playful pat.

Brian shouldn't have been surprised by the talk. He had moved up the ladder pretty quickly at WBTN and though he wanted to believe it was because of his journalistic abilities, he suspected that it had a lot to do with his looks. The demographics said it all. He was the most popular newsperson in the entire city with women aged twenty-one through forty-nine. And his numbers with the male audience weren't too bad either. The women in focus groups liked the way he looked and men liked that he was just a regular guy from Southie. The people of Boston trusted Brian Quinn to tell them the truth.

"I may have the face, but not the stomach for it. Any more than you'd be able to handle standing behind a studio camera. You're like me. You like to be out on the streets."

"But if you don't want the promotion, why do you work so hard?"

Brian shrugged. "Because I like to be the first to know."

"Taneesha! We've got a three-alarm fire in Dorchester. You're up."

Taneesha turned and waved at one of the junior reporters who was racing toward the door. "Let's go, then." She gave Brian a smile. "When you break this story, don't you forget your favorite camera goddess. I'll stick that camera so far up Patterson's nose, we'll be able to read his mind."

"You'll be there," Brian replied. He watched as Taneesha hurried off to the waiting news truck, then opened his desk drawer and pulled out the handheld tape recorder. He popped in a new tape, pausing to think about what Taneesha had said.

He knew that management had plans for him, that he was fast becoming "the new face of WBTN-TV." And until this moment, he'd been caught up in all the excitement of his meteoric rise. But Brian knew what he wanted and it wasn't an anchor job, even if it meant big money and a high profile in town. All he really cared about was telling a good story.

When he'd gotten out of college, he'd been determined to work in print journalism. So he'd paid his dues with small newspapers in Connecticut and Vermont. But he'd wanted to get back to Boston and when he'd been offered an entry-level news-writing job at WBTN, he'd taken it. He'd never once expected it to blossom into the career it had.

Brian slipped the tape recorder into his jacket, then pulled his car keys out of his trouser pocket. As he headed toward the door, Taneesha's warning still niggled at his brain. He'd worked with her for over a year and she'd never steered him wrong—when it came to a story or personal advice. But every instinct told him that, contrary to public opinion, his career wasn't headed in the right direction. And Brian trusted his instincts.

Hell, he could just quit right now and start over again, find a job at a decent newspaper and work his way up. But he was thirty years old. At that age, a guy was supposed to have his life in order, his priorities straight. But then, he hadn't been brought up in a conventional family, so maybe he had a good excuse.

Life in the Quinn house had taught all six of the Quinn brothers to live from moment to moment. Their father, Seamus, was rarely at home, his job as a commercial fisherman keeping him away from Southie for weeks at a time. And Brian's mother had left the family when Brian was only three years old. He and his brothers had raised themselves, with oldest brother Conor serving as the parental figure.

They'd all gotten in their share of trouble, but Brian and his twin, Sean, had been the wildest. They'd managed to compile a rather impressive record of petty crimes with the police, but luckily, by the time the trouble got serious, Conor had begun working as a cop. He'd thrown them in jail for three days after they'd stolen a neighbor's car, then made them spend the summer painting the guy's house as punishment. The neighbor was happy to have the help and Brian and Sean decided that a life of crime truly didn't pay.

So Brian turned his energies to his studies and took a part-time job loading newspapers on the trucks at the *Globe.* And when he graduated from high school, he became the second Quinn to attend college after his older brother, Brendan. When he registered, he'd been asked to declare a major and asked the pretty girl next to him in line what she was majoring in. Journalism had simply been a fallback position, but it had been the best place to meet passionate girls, short of the nursing program. And the classes had been surprisingly interesting, especially when he discovered he had a knack for constructing a story.

Brian jogged to his car in the station parking lot. If he was lucky, he'd get what he needed early in the evening and he could spend the rest of his Saturday night at Quinn's Pub, relaxing over a pint of Guinness and charming a few good-looking women. Brian chuckled. Maybe he'd even wear the tux. Though it probably meant at least an hour's worth of good-natured ribbing, he'd at least have his pick of the beauties in the bar.

"First business, then pleasure," he murmured as he started the car.

BY THE TIME THE TABLES were cleared and the band began playing, Lily Gallagher was ready to go home—or back to her hotel, which was home for now. She leaned on the bar and ordered her first glass of champagne, then winced at her sore feet, chiding herself on her choice of footwear. Though the strappy designer shoes went perfectly with her gown, they weren't made for a long evening on her feet.

She'd flown into Boston just that afternoon from Chicago, curious as to the reasons she'd been summoned. Richard Patterson had personally contacted her boss at DeLay Scoville Public Relations and requested her services. According to Don DeLay, Richard Patterson was willing to toss down a hefty retainer without any explanation of what he wanted her for.

Lily wasn't about to refuse. A job like this was her ticket to the top, just one step away from a vice presidency and a corner office. And right now, that office was in her sights. Though nothing had been explained up front, Lily suspected why she'd been the chosen one. Patterson was a big real estate developer and just last year she'd handled a huge scandal with a real estate developer in Chicago.

Crisis public relations was her specialty. People called her when things went bad and it was her job to make them better. On the plane trip from Chicago, Lily had read everything she could about Patterson Properties and Investments, a company that owned shopping malls and motels and fast-food restaurants. Richard Patterson was well-connected politically and was slowly climbing the social ladder in Boston, despite his humble beginnings in a working-class Boston neighborhood.

For Lily, it had been a relief to be offered a job outside of Chicago, though she missed her new house and her best friend, Emma Carsten. She and Emma worked together at the agency and often talked about breaking out and starting a company of their own. But the practicalities of paying a mortgage had made a promotion at DeLay the primary goal for the moment.

Hopefully, Richard Patterson would have some juicy crisis that she could sink her teeth into, some touchy political problem or maybe a community relations issue that she could solve. She'd fix what needed fixing and have a nice addition to her portfolio when she went back to Chicago in a few months. Then she could demand that promotion.

"Lily?"

She turned to find Richard Patterson standing behind her. He was a handsome, forty-something guy with graying temples and impeccable grooming. He wore a beautifully tailored tuxedo, probably from one of the best menswear designers. If he hadn't been a client—and he hadn't been married—Lily might have considered him a possibility. But she never mixed business with pleasure. "The party is wonderful," she said. "You've done a terrific job as chairman, Mr. Patterson."

He forced a tight smile. "I didn't do anything. I hired a party planner and my wife took care of the rest. Listen, I have to leave. I've got a flight to catch. An emergency with a group of investors from Japan. I know we haven't had a chance to talk and I'll be out of town for the next few days. But I want you to call my secretary on Monday. She'll set up appointments with my key management people. You'll be up to speed when I get back."

"Good. I need to know everything I can. Maybe if you tell me what you'd like me to work on, I can get a head start and when we meet I—"

"We'll discuss that on Tuesday," he interrupted, glancing over his shoulder.

"All right."

"If there's anything you need, call Mrs. Wilburn. Boston is beautiful in the month of June. Get out and see some of the sights." With that, he turned and strode away, leaving Lily to wonder why it had been so important for her to arrive today—and to attend this party.

Lily glanced around, deciding that she'd wait until she was sure Richard was gone and then call it a night.

She took another sip of her champagne as she studied the couples on the dance floor. The ballroom at the Copley Plaza was beautifully decorated to look like the gardens at Versailles. Fountains trickled and arbors were laced with heavily-scented flowers and tiny white lights making an incredibly romantic scene. She sighed softly.

There were other reasons she was glad to leave Chicago. Her engagement to attorney Daniel Martin was now officially off. After two years of dating and a four-month engagement, she'd thought she'd finally found the man of her dreams—until she'd discovered him naked and in bed with an exotic-looking brunette and her two artificially enhanced breasts. She'd never expected him to sink to such depths and his only excuse had been that he just wasn't ready to commit.

Lily had planned her life around this man, had invested her future with him, and suddenly it was over and she had been forced back to square one in her personal life—forced to admit that she'd surrendered far too much for love. Sometimes Chicago felt like a desert for single women. Plenty of great-looking men on the horizon, but when you got too close, they were simply a mirage, a figment of a desperate imagination.

She took another sip of her champagne and glanced around the room. Maybe it was time to stop being desperate, to quit looking so hard for love and just settle for...a little lust. She'd made the first move toward independence, buying a house of her own. "I know exactly what I need now," Lily murmured. "A nice, tidy, but very passionate, one-night stand."

She hadn't gone looking for creeps and jerks, but the men who wandered into her life had always been strangely unavailable—engaged to someone who didn't understand, married to a woman they'd forgotten to mention, emotionally cold, commitment-phobic, fascinated with ladies' footwear, contemplating a change in sexual preference, and then Daniel, a unrepentant philanderer. She'd even tried to make a bicoastal relationship work with a Los Angeles writer which racked up an impressive number of frequent-flyer miles but ended with him falling in love with a vapid starlet.

But now she had an opportunity to have a man on her terms. She was the unavailable, commitment-phobic party, living and working in Boston for only a few months, uninterested in a long-term relationship. She could play the field, have a little fun and avoid all the messy strings that seemed to keep two people tied together for far too long.

Lily sighed. This fund-raiser was the last place she'd find a single man. The only reason men attended a charity event was that their wives insisted. In truth, most of the men in attendance probably didn't want to be there at all. Lily had always wanted to plan an "un" event. An imaginary charity dinner and dance that people paid *not* to attend. Then all the money could go to charity rather than to overblown decorations and overpriced *foie gras* and over-the-top designer gowns.

She quickly snatched another glass of champagne from a passing waiter and stared up at the balconies, deciding to find a table on the second level where she could observe the party in peace. A few minutes later, she settled down in a quiet corner on the opposite end from the dance band. She kicked off her shoes and rubbed her feet together, finally feeling a nice buzz from the champagne she'd gulped down. A waiter stopped at her table and offered her another glass and she took it and set it across from her, as if she were expecting someone to join her.

"A woman as beautiful as you shouldn't be sitting here alone."

Lily's gaze slowly rose to a man standing beside her table, wondering at her luck. But though he was attractive enough, his smile was just a little too...practiced. His dark hair was slicked back and he wore an ill-fitting tuxedo. Still, she decided to at least give him a chance. "Actually, I'm fine," she said.

He pulled out the chair across from her and sat down, despite the champagne goblet. "Well, I'm not," he said. "I'm here alone and everyone else is here with a significant other. I'm Jim Franklin."

"I'm Lily," she said.

"Just Lily?"

"Lily Gallagher."

"Well, Lily Gallagher, since we both seem to be alone here, maybe we can be alone together. Tell me about yourself."

Lily opened her mouth to respond, but Jim Franklin didn't wait for an answer. "I'm an investment analyst with Bardwell Fleming. Let me tell you, these parties are a great investment. My bosses buy a spot at the table and then send us guys in to drum up some business. We don't sell stocks and bonds, but we offer analysis services for all types of investments. I've lived in Boston for about five years. Got transferred up here from our New York office."

After all her bravado, when it came down to it, lust was a tricky thing. Either a girl felt it or she didn't. And

Lily already knew that this was a guy who didn't make her pulse pound.

"So, what do you do, Lily?"

"Mr. Franklin, I'm really not—"

"Jim," he insisted. "Do you have a retirement plan? Have you invested your money wisely?"

Lily grabbed her glass and drained it, then quickly stood. "I'm just going to get myself some more champagne. If you'll excuse—"

"And here's a waiter now," Franklin said, flashing her a blinding smile.

Lily bit back a curse and sat down again. If this wasn't pure torture, she didn't know what was. It wasn't her habit to be rude, especially in a business situation, but she doubted that Richard Patterson was friends with Jim Franklin, investment analyst.

As Franklin prattled on about liquid assets and high-yield bonds, Lily let her gaze wander, interjecting a word every now and then to answer one of Franklin's questions, before he resumed his Wall Street chatter. She pasted a bland smile on her face and fixed her gaze just over his right shoulder, wondering how long she'd be obligated to carry on this one-sided conversation. Her mind scrambled for an excuse, something that would politely put him off. Then she noticed a man standing behind Franklin, his shoulder braced against a marble column, an amused grin twitching his lips.

Lily quickly glanced away, but when she looked back, she found him still staring at her. Then he looked at his watch and pretended to yawn and Lily couldn't help but smile. She took another sip of her champagne and observed the man from over the rim of the glass.

Unlike Jim Franklin, this guy was downright gorgeous. He had dark hair, just long enough to brush his collar but perfectly trimmed. Dark brows accented eyes of an indeterminate shade, but Lily knew they were probably some uncommon and very arresting color. Her gaze skimmed over his body, finding him taller than average and beautifully built, his tailored tux accenting wide shoulders and a narrow waist.

When she returned to his face, his smile was a bit wider. He nodded at her, as if he knew exactly what she was thinking. And then he pushed away from the column and started toward her. Lily held her breath, her eyes still fixed on his, her heart beating a little faster.

"Sweetheart," he said, stopping next to the table. "I've been looking all over for you."

He reached out and Lily hesitantly placed her hand in his. But to her surprise, he drew it up and placed a kiss near her wrist. She swallowed hard. "Darling," she said. "You're late."

"Not too late, I hope. You will forgive me, won't you?"

She slowly stood. "Of course." Lily glanced over at Jim Franklin as she grabbed her shoes from the floor. "Thanks for the investment advice, Jim. Have fun at the party."

The stranger tucked her hand in the crook of his arm and started toward the nearest exit. When they reached the hall, he stopped. "You're safe now."

"I wasn't really in any danger," Lily said. "Unless boredom is fatal."

"With a guy like that, you never know. I wasn't willing to watch you throw yourself over the railing just to get away from him."

"Thanks for saving me," Lily said.

"No problem. So, are you here alone? Or did your date desert you?" He paused. "Or maybe that was your date?"

Lily shook her head. "I'm here alone. A professional obligation."

"And when is that obligation finished?" he asked.

"Right now." Lily smiled hesitantly, realizing that she might have given him the wrong idea. Suddenly, she wasn't interested in going back to the hotel. She'd just met an attractive, sexy, and witty man—a rare occurrence in her life. "What about you? I suppose you have a reason for being here—besides rescuing me from the scintillating Mr. Franklin."

He chuckled. "Actually, I crashed the party. The band sounded good so I thought I'd check it out. But the crowd was a little bit too stuffy for me...until I saw you." He let his gaze rake over her body and Lily shivered. "Has anyone told you that you look incredible in that dress?"

"You flatter me," she teased, keeping the banter light. "And I don't even know your name."

"Oh, let's not play that game. And let's not talk about what we do for a living. Or where we come from. And the weather is off-limits, too."

"All right," Lily said, intrigued by the game. "We can talk about art and literature and music. But I have to call you something."

"Darling was kind of nice," he said with a devilish grin.

"I guess you can call me sweetheart, then," Lily countered. Though their conversation had a provocative tone, she couldn't help but giggle. From the amused expression on his handsome face, he wasn't taking this any more seriously than she was.

"Sweetie for short," he said. "Come on, sweetie, they're playing our song. I think we should dance, don't you?" He took the shoes from her hand, flipped them over his shoulder and sauntered toward the stairs.

Lily watched him for a long moment, her gaze fixed on his wide shoulders. Why not enjoy this handsome stranger for a night and leave it at that? She'd hoped to find a man in Boston and this stranger certainly fit the bill. And if she admitted up front that there was no possibility for a real relationship, then she couldn't get hurt again.

He stopped walking and glanced over his shoulder. "Are you coming, darling?"

Lily laughed softly before she picked up her skirts and hurried after him. "Have you forgotten my name already? I'm sweetheart. You're darling."

THE BAND HAD JUST BEGUN their rendition of "Isn't It Romantic" when Brian drew the beautiful stranger in the gold gown out onto the dance floor. He twirled her beneath his arm and then pulled her against his body, moving along with the music. Her gown dipped low on her back and he spread his palm over her warm skin, surprised at how soft it felt.

The evening had quickly turned from business to pleasure. When he'd arrived, he'd easily talked his way inside without an invitation, but the opportunity to confront Richard Patterson hadn't materialized. According to one of the guests, Patterson had left a few minutes before due to some business emergency. Brian had decided to check out the crowd from the balcony in hopes that he might spot some of Patterson's cronies. But once he'd set eyes on the girl in the gold dress, he'd pretty much forgotten about everything else.

"You're a very good dancer," she said.

"And you are, too," he returned.

He found their little game endlessly intriguing. But he wasn't sure where the game ended and reality began. She acted as if she didn't recognize him and with his face on billboards and busboards all over town, that was a bit difficult to believe. Maybe she didn't watch the news. Or maybe she didn't live in Boston.

He was willing to play along, at least for the time being. Though he'd seduced his fair share of women before, he'd always taken a straightforward approach to the matter. But this was different. They'd constructed a silly set of rules. Were the rules there to protect them both from their desires—or to liberate them from their inhibitions?

"I took dance lessons from age seven to age twelve," Lily said. "My mother insisted. She said I'd need it someday and I didn't believe her. I guess I was wrong." She smoothed her hand over his shoulder. "And how about you?"

"I just have natural grace and athletic ability. Plus, you're making me look a whole lot better than I really am."

Brian looked down at her and couldn't take his eyes off her face. She was beautiful, with lively green eyes and a riot of auburn curls cascading from the crown of her head. Little tendrils had escaped the mass of curls and caressed her cheeks and forehead and Brian fought the urge to brush them away.

But then he realized there was no need to just contemplate touching her. Nothing in her manner made him believe his touch would be unwelcome. He reached up and smoothed his fingers along her cheekbone, tucking the strands behind her ear. For a moment, her breath stilled and their gazes locked. And then he grabbed her around the waist. "Dip," he said, leaning her back.

They continued to dance, whirling around the floor as if they were Ginger Rogers and Fred Astaire. In truth, Brian was surprised at how easy it was to have her in his arms. She seemed to anticipate his every move. With her, he did look like the best dancer on the floor. And in his eyes, she was the most beautiful woman in the room.

"So if we don't talk about our jobs, or the weather or where we're from, what should we talk about?" she asked.

"Whatever you want," Brian said. "I'll give you five questions and you give me five. Anything. No restrictions. And we have to answer honestly. That should start some interesting conversation, don't you think?"

"I'll start," she said. "Are you married?"

"No. Never been married. Are you?"

"No, never." The orchestra segued into "Embraceable You" and they continued to dance. "I came close once, but it didn't work." She considered her next question carefully. "Involved?" she asked.

He clucked his tongue and shook his head. "Oh, sweetie, you're going to burn a question on that? No, I'm not involved. And I won't ask you that one, because I don't care if you are involved. You're here with me now, and that's all that matters."

"One more question," she said. "What's your name?"

"Brian," he said. "Brian Quinn." He paused, waiting for her to offer her own name, then realized she was going to force him to ask. "And what about you?"

"It's Lily Gallagher. That's three for me, and two for you. Don't you want to ask me another question?"

"Are you from Boston?" he asked, unable to contain his curiosity.

"For the time being. But I live in Chicago."

So she really didn't know who he was. They were essentially strangers. "It's nice to meet you, Lily," he murmured. "Lily. I like that name. It suits you."

"And why is that?" She winced. "And that wasn't one of my five questions. Just curiosity."

"Oh, now here's the test for me. I'm going to have to come up with something very poetic to say about your name or you'll realize that I'm not as smooth as I'm pretending to be."

"I'm a big fan of poetry, Brian Quinn."

He cleared his throat. "Well, unless it's a dirty limerick, I think you're out of luck with me."

"Hey, I'll take a limerick."

Brian groaned softly. "I guess I stepped in that one." He thought for a moment, all the off-color limericks he'd ever heard racing though his mind. "I'm Irish, so this could come naturally. There once was a girl dressed in gold, who I approached in a way very bold. We danced through the night, held each other so tight, and left all our sad stories untold."

Lily laughed. "That wasn't bad. But it didn't answer the question."

"That's because the only words that rhyme with Lily are filly, frilly and dilly." He paused, studying her until she was forced to avert her gaze. "Lily suits you because I like the sound of it when I say it. And I don't think I've ever met anyone named Lily, so whenever I hear that name, I'll think of you first."

A tiny sigh slipped from her lips. "That's very poetic."

He stared down at her, his gaze skimming over her pretty features. He didn't have to think before he kissed her. He simply leaned forward and she was there, waiting, her upturned mouth soft and damp and sweet. There was no hesitation and no doubt that it was the best use of that particular moment. And then he drew away and they continued dancing.

She felt good in his arms, as if she fit. His hand rested on her back in just the right spot and her fingers nestled perfectly in his palm. And their bodies brushed against each other as he pulled her near, hips against hips, her breasts pressed to his chest.

Brian couldn't remember the first time he'd been attracted to the opposite sex. It had happened so long ago and there had been so many girls and women since then. But there was something different about Lily, something that he couldn't put his finger on. Maybe it was the little game they were playing, two strangers in the night exchanging more than glances.

With each new tune the orchestra played, he learned more about her, about the way she moved and the sound of her voice, the shape of her body beneath her dress and the smell of her perfume in the curve of her neck. They talked, but not about anything important, yet each word seemed to draw him in, to make him want her more. He didn't know what she did for a living, he didn't know her favorite food or even if she had any hobbies.

But he did know where the evening might end and for the first time in his adult life, Brian wasn't sure that he wanted it to end there. He pushed the thoughts from his head, focusing on the music and scent of her hair, determined to enjoy each little moment, without regard to where it was leading.

He drew in a slow breath. Hell, that was a revelation. Maybe spending time with a woman didn't always have to be about sex. Maybe seduction could end in just a simple kiss good-night.

The music stopped and the lights in the ballroom gradually came up. Lily lifted her head from his shoulder and glanced around, her brow furrowed. "What time is it?"

"Time to go," he said. "We're the last people on the dance floor."

A faint blush crept up her cheeks. Even in the harsh light, she looked beautiful. "I didn't realize it was so late."

Brian slipped his arm around her waist and steered her toward the table where she'd left her shoes and her purse. "Let's get out of here." He picked up her shoes and bent down, helping her slip them on, then fumbling with the straps.

They started toward the lobby, but halfway there, Brian pulled her into a small alcove and kissed her, her damp lips just too tempting to resist. His hands smoothed over her face as his tongue invaded her mouth. A tiny sigh slipped from her throat and when he finally drew away, she didn't open her eyes for a long time.

"Where are we going?" she murmured.

"I don't know. Anywhere. As long as it's with you."

"I—I have a car outside," she offered.

"Let's go."

When they got to the street, Lily handed the parking attendant a card. He made a quick phone call and a few seconds later a limo pulled up to the curb.

Brian ignored the car until Lily started toward it. The parking attendant held open the door and she slipped inside, then looked back out at Brian.

"When you said car, I figured you meant Toyota or Ford," he said.

"It's a limo," she called, leaning out the door.

"I can see that," he said, getting inside.

"Do you want to take your car?"

Brian thought about the beat-up Chevy parked in a public lot a few blocks away and compared it to the luxurious leather interior. "No, this will do just fine."

"Where to?" the chauffeur asked, watching them in the rearview mirror.

Brian looked at Lily, deciding to leave it up to her. "Where would you like to go?" he asked softly, his gaze fixed on her lips.

"Just drive," she murmured, wrapping her arms around his neck. "Take us to see the sights."

The privacy screen whirred as it rose, but all Brian could really hear was the thud of his heart as he pulled Lily into his arms.

2

HE PRESSED HER BACK into the soft leather seats, pulling her body beneath his, his mouth covering hers in a deep kiss. Lily moaned softly, her head spinning with the taste of him, her hands running over his body frantically. She knew she ought to stop, that she should want to stop. This was crazy!

She'd just met him a few hours before, but from the moment he'd looked at her, she'd been captivated, every nerve in her body jangling with anticipation. Lily shoved her hands beneath his jacket, pushing it over his shoulders. With a low groan, Brian tugged it off, his lips never leaving hers.

Lily knew if she asked him to stop, he would. There was something about Brian Quinn that she trusted, even if her instincts told her to be careful. But she didn't want to stop. As long as they stayed in the limo with the driver on the other side of the glass, then she'd be in complete control.

As her fingers fumbled with his bow tie, Lily felt her heart begin to race. This instant attraction they felt for each other was too much to deny. It was powerful, magnetic, an unseen force that seemed to propel them closer and closer to intimacy. She should be able to resist, but with every kiss and every touch, her inhibitions dissolved.

Was this really what she wanted, to throw herself

into the arms of a stranger simply to satisfy a craving? His hands skimmed over the bodice of her dress and grasped her hips, pulling her close. *Yes*, Lily's brain screamed. *Yes, yes, yes.*

As he drew her beneath him, the fabric of her wide skirt billowed around them, creating a barrier as effective as any chastity belt. He stilled his frenetic exploration of her clothing, cursing softly. "What are you hiding under there?"

Lily giggled. "If I would have known I'd end up here, I would have chosen a different dress." Something shorter, with buttons down the front, she mused.

Brian grinned, then glanced out the window. "The Public Garden," he murmured. "And Boston Common is coming up. There's a statue of George Washington that you might be interested in seeing."

"Forget the sights," Lily said, grabbing the front of his pleated shirt and dragging him back down. "I'll see them later."

His gaze raked over her features and settled on her lips. "Lily, are you trying to seduce me?"

"If you have to ask, then I guess I'm doing a pretty poor job of it." Lily sighed. "I've never really seduced a man before."

Brian smoothed his palm over her cheek, then let it drift down her neck. "Believe me, you're doing just fine." He slipped his fingers under the spaghetti strap of her gown, toyed with it for a moment and pushed it off her shoulder. "Tell me what you want," he murmured as he pressed his mouth to her collarbone.

"That's nice," she said. He let his hand drift down further until his fingers brushed along the swell of her breast. She sucked in a sharp breath. "Oh, and that's nice, too."

"Tell me," he urged, running his fingers along the edge of her dress, back and forth in a lazy caress. Her skin began to tingle and Lily closed her eyes and arched up, bracing herself on her elbows. Suddenly, she wasn't the person in charge of this seduction, he was. "I want your hands on my body," she whispered as her inhibitions slowly dissolved.

She felt his hands circle her waist and then, in one easy movement, he pulled her up to sit on the seat across from him. Her skirts billowed up around them, but he brushed them aside and took her foot in his hand. "I was beginning to wonder if you had legs underneath this skirt." He slipped her left shoe off and gently massaged her foot.

Lily moaned softly, leaning back into the seat. When she'd asked him to touch her, she hadn't had a foot massage in mind. But as he rubbed his thumbs into the arch of her foot, she was surprised at how sensual the caress was—especially when he set her foot between his legs and slid his hands up her calf.

Her foot rested in a very intimate spot, and every time he moved, it rubbed against his growing erection. Lily had never considered the sole of her foot to be an erogenous zone, but as his hands traveled upward to her knees and then her thighs, she knew she'd be learning a few things about seduction from Brian Quinn.

Lily wondered where they'd stop—or whether they'd stop at all. Since she couldn't see what he was doing beneath her dress, she closed her eyes and enjoyed the sensation of his warm palms on her skin.

And when he moved to her inner thighs, she held her breath. "Look at that," he murmured.

Lily opened her eyes.

"Park Street Church," he said, nodding toward the window. "The tall steeple just over there. And the Boston Athenaeum and the Old Granary Burying Ground. Lots of famous Revolutionary War soldiers are buried there." His hand slid a bit higher and Lily sucked in a sharp breath. "Including Paul Revere." And then he was moving again, running his fingers up and over her hips. He caught the lace of her panties with his fingers and slowly began to tug them down. Lily shifted and they slipped to her knees and then off her feet.

Brian held them up and examined the lacy scrap of lingerie. "I love black underwear."

Lily leaned forward, but her skirts once again billowed up between them. She shoved the fabric down, then knelt in front of him. Though he'd lost his jacket and tie, his shirt was still buttoned to the neck. With nimble fingers, Lily reached out and began to work on the studs.

When she'd brushed the shirt aside, she smoothed her hands over his chest, hard and muscular. Then she leaned forward and pressed her lips to the soft dusting of hair beneath his collarbone. Working her way down, she kissed a trail to his belly. But when she let her fingers drop to his trousers, Brian grabbed her hands and drew them away.

"Are you sure about this, Lily?"

She smiled. He didn't have to be such a gentleman, but Lily was glad that he made the attempt. "There's nothing wrong with two..." She moved back to his trousers. "Consenting adults..." She worked the button open. "Engaging in mutually satisfying..." She slowly drew the zipper down. "Sex."

Most guys had probably dreamed about hearing those very words. And Lily had never expected that she might be the one to say them. But she'd had enough of "relationships." What was wrong with taking pleasure where she found it? She'd always wanted to make more out of a simple sexual attraction and that had only led to disappointment.

Lily knew Brian Quinn wouldn't disappoint her. Not tonight. And after tonight, she wouldn't give him a chance. They'd go their separate ways and be satisfied with the pleasure they'd taken in each other. "Haven't you ever just been swept away by the moment?" she asked.

"Yeah," he said with a smile. "I think that's happening right now."

He reached around her back and pulled on the zipper of her gown. When it gaped in front, Brian drew Lily up onto his lap, settling her knees on either side of his legs. She groaned as he unhooked her strapless bra and tossed it aside.

He reached up and shut off the light, the sights of Boston now illuminating the tinted windows of the limo and their tempting seduction. Brian slowly explored her body with his hands and his lips. Every so often, he'd brush aside clothes to get to naked skin, but both of them still remained half-dressed, their clothes providing an effective barrier to complete surrender.

Lily wrapped her arms around his neck as he slipped his hands beneath her skirts. He'd done away with her underwear and now she was naked beneath the gown, the fabric shifting over her skin as she moved. He drew her down, settling her on his lap, but his boxers still stood between them and pure contact.

She reached between them and tugged at the silk, but Brian whispered for her to stop. He searched the car for his jacket at the same time she looked for her purse. Lily found a condom first and handed it to him. He smiled gratefully. "For a minute there I was afraid we'd have to stop at a drugstore."

Lily pushed up, anticipating the feel of him slipping inside of her. Then she slowly lowered herself on top of him, his hard shaft probing at her damp core. Brian moaned softly, his hands sliding up beneath her skirt to her hips. He held her fast, controlling her movement until he was completely buried inside of her.

She'd only met him a few hours ago and now, they were making love in the back of a limo. Just the thought of it made her shiver with desire. This was what it was all about, basic lust, the need to be with a man, to feel him move inside of her and to reach her release.

But as they moved, Lily couldn't help but believe there was something more to this spontaneous intimacy. Maybe she had fallen a little in love with Brian over the course of the evening. He was sweet and funny and sexy and he'd swept her off her feet. She couldn't have chosen a more perfect man for this little adventure.

Lily ran her hands over his face. He opened his eyes and looked up at her. Their gazes locked as he began to increase their rhythm. She watched his reactions as his hands controlled her, the pleasure that suffused his features, first easy and then intense. He drew her up and down on top of him but then stopped suddenly.

Without warning, he held on to her waist and gently laid her back onto the seat. Her skirt billowed up around her face and he fought through it until he could kiss her.

He was so gentle with her, yet so determined, and when he slipped his hand between them and touched her, Lily knew that he be wouldn't satisfied with simply taking his own pleasure. He began to move again as he caressed her. A tremor shot through her at his touch and she felt her need increase, tightening in her belly.

Lily closed her eyes and focused on that feeling, on the sweet sensations that raced through her limbs to the tips of her fingers and toes. Every thought dissolved in her head and she could only feel, aching for her release. She arched up, meeting his every thrust, daring him to take everything she offered.

His name slipped from her lips, not once, but twice and then again, a plea to give her more.

"Come with me," he murmured, his mouth hot on hers. "Come with me, now."

And then, as if his invitation was all she was waiting for, Lily felt her body explode in a soul-shattering orgasm. She cried out, but he'd already found his own release, driving into her one last time and then allowing the spasms to shake his body.

He collapsed on top of her, then rolled off to the side, grasping her waist to pull her tightly against him. For a long time, he didn't speak and Lily listened to his breathing, harsh and quick at first, then slowing.

"Are you all right?" she asked.

"I can't believe we just did that. I've never...well, I've just never done that."

Lily smiled hesitantly. "I find that a little hard to believe."

"Believe it," Brian said, nuzzling her neck. "That was pretty incredible. You were...wow."

She furrowed her fingers through his hair and kissed him, lingering for a long time. Lily had never felt so completely satisfied and given the choice, she'd have spent the next week making love to Brian Quinn in the back seat of the limo. But she'd made a promise to herself and she was going to keep it. A one-night stand was just that—one night.

Suddenly, a wave of regret washed over her. Maybe this hadn't been such a good idea. After what they'd shared, Lily didn't want to just walk away. Brian Quinn was a wonderful man! And from what she could tell, he was available. She sucked in a sharp breath. Now was not the time to change directions.

"I think I have two questions left, don't I?" Brian murmured.

Dragged from her thoughts, Lily frowned. "I—I don't know. I lost count."

"So what happens now?" Brian asked, running his hand along her shoulder. "We can't drive around in this limo forever. We're going to run out of gas."

"I say we go until we run out of gas," Lily murmured, her attention fixed on his mouth.

"We could go to my place or we could go to yours," he suggested.

Again, Lily had to force herself to remember her plan against formidable distractions. She sat up and adjusted her dress, then reached for the zipper. Brian turned her around on the seat and zipped it for her, then let his hands drift down her arms.

His touch sent a shiver through her, but Lily occupied herself by collecting her underwear and shoes. She stuffed her panties and bra into her purse, and slipped the strappy sandals on her feet. Then she pressed the intercom button. "Driver, take us back to the Copley Plaza, please." She glanced over her shoulder and her gaze met his. For a moment she lost herself in the beautiful color of his eyes. "Let's be honest with each other," she murmured. "This was all about passion and lust and it was wonderful. It was exciting. But it doesn't have to be more than that. I don't expect more."

"But we should at least—"

Lily placed her finger on his lips. "What? I should give you my phone number and we'll get together? Maybe you'll call, but maybe, after thinking about it for a day or two, you'll decide that it's better to just let it go. But if I give you my phone number, then maybe I'll expect you to call and when you don't, I'll be hurt. Or maybe we'll get together again and realize that there's nothing but...*this* between us. Or maybe, we'll even find that we have a lot in common and we'll have a relationship. But then, you'll grow bored or I'll get too demanding and we'll fight and it will all end badly and we'll hate each other." Lily smiled and drew in a deep breath. "So maybe it's best that I don't give you my phone number and we just skip all that pain and heartbreak."

He buttoned his pants and yanked up the zipper, then reached for his jacket. "Lily, I don't—"

This time she replaced her finger with her mouth, kissing him deeply, her arms wrapped around his neck. "I had a wonderful time, darling."

He sighed. "So did I, sweetheart," he murmured, pressing his mouth into the curve of her neck. "But, that doesn't mean—"

"Yes, it does."

The car stopped and Lily looked out the window, surprised to find that they were back at the Plaza so quickly. Brian slipped his hand around her nape and drew her close, giving her a fierce kiss designed to persuade her to go with his point of view. "Won't you at least let me try to change your mind?" She drew away, shaking her head and he finally loosened his grip. "Then, I guess I won't be seeing you again."

"I guess you won't," Lily said with a smile. "I had a good time, Brian."

He looked into her eyes for a long moment, then shrugged and slid across the seat to the door. "Good night, Lily."

"Goodbye, Brian."

With that, he pushed the door open and stepped out. For a moment, Lily thought he might turn around and say something to her. But then he shut the door. She watched him walk down the sidewalk, but the tinted windows made that difficult. With a soft sigh, Lily sank back into the leather seat and pressed her palm to her chest. "What have I done?"

"Miss Gallagher?"

Startled, Lily pushed the intercom button. "Please take me back to my hotel."

As the car pulled away from the curb, Lily closed her eyes and tipped her head back. This was no time for doubts. She had a job to do here in Boston and when she was finished, she'd go home to Chicago. And she'd take along incredible memories of a very passionate and spontaneous encounter to keep her warm at night.

She braced her hands on the seat and her fingers fell on a smooth bit of fabric. Lily picked it up and realized it was Brian's bow tie.

"It was great sex," Lily murmured, fingering the tie. "And that's all it was." But though she said the words, they just didn't seem to ring true.

"AREN'T YOU DOING the news tonight?"

Brian slid onto a bar stool next to his twin brother Sean and waved to his father at the far end of the bar. For a Sunday evening, Quinn's Pub in South Boston was relatively empty. A few of the regulars were playing pool in the back and a couple sat in one of the booths near the bar. A soft Irish ballad played from the jukebox.

Seamus, a canvas apron around his waist, strolled up and tossed a paper coaster in front of Brian. "Aren't you doing the news tonight? We're tuned in," he said, pointing to the television in the corner.

Brian nodded. "Yeah. The eleven o'clock news. I've got to be at the station at seven. I thought I'd get something to eat."

"We've got corned beef and cabbage," Seamus said. "I'll get you a plate."

"No cabbage," Brian said. "It'll make me burp."

Seamus raised a bushy white eyebrow. "So?"

"Da, I have to read the news. I can't be burping every few seconds. Give me a club soda over ice. And a cheeseburger, no onions."

Seamus fetched the drink, then wrote the order

down on a pad and walked it back to Henry, the short-order cook in the kitchen.

Brian and Sean sat silently, both of them contemplating their drinks. They didn't need to talk. Since the moment they'd been born, they'd shared a silent kind of communication, an ability to read each other's moods, to know what the other was thinking. While Sean rarely confided in his other brothers—or anyone for that matter—when he was alone with Brian, he was able to open up.

Brian knew everyone thought Sean was shy and aloof. But he also knew his twin brother used an indifferent facade to hide a deeply sensitive nature. He wrapped himself in a protective armor, allowing very few people to see the man underneath.

Of all of the Quinn brothers, Sean had been the one who'd come away with the most childhood scars. He'd been the one to rebel against his circumstances. He'd never really learned to trust and had turned into a brooding loner. He'd washed out of the police academy and drifted into private investigative work. It had been a good choice for Sean, but it hadn't made him any more outgoing.

"How's business?" Brian asked.

"Not bad. Not good, either."

"I thought you made a bundle on that case with Liam and Eleanor and that Pettibone guy."

A few months back, Sean had taken on an embezzlement case for a Manhattan bank and enlisted the aid of their youngest brother, Liam. Charged with surveillance on the female suspect, Liam had fallen in love with the woman. After they had cleared her name, he and Eleanor Thorpe had continued seeing each other and announced their engagement the day after Brendan and Amy's wedding in early May.

"I did," Sean said. "But I burned it all on expenses on another big case. My rich client didn't like what I found. Turns out his wife wasn't cheating. He's decided not to pay the bill. Now, I've got to spend more money to get him to pay. I've got to hire a lawyer and file a lawsuit."

"Sorry," Brian murmured. "I wish I had something I could throw your way."

Sean held up his hand. "I'm going to be fine. Liam's making money now. He's paying the rent at our place—for once. He and Ellie are moving out at the end of the summer. I'll be all right until then."

"How is that, living with them both?"

Sean shrugged. "She likes to clean. She's got a thing about the toilet seat. And I really wish she wouldn't hang her...underthings all over the bathroom."

"Yeah, I suppose that is a little distracting," he murmured, his mind flashing an image of Lily Gallagher's lingerie, that strapless number made of black lace and the matching panties. He drew a sharp breath and pushed the image out of his head. He'd spent the entire day thinking about Lily and it was time he quit! Yes, she was beautiful and intriguing and the night they'd spent together had been unforgettable, but he knew better than to make it into something more than it was.

"She likes to cook," Sean continued. "There are always leftovers in the fridge." He shrugged and took another sip of his Guinness. "Between eating at the pub and eating at home, I've been saving a lot of money on food."

Brian nodded. He stared down the length of the bar

and caught the glances sent their way by a pair of cur-
vaceous blondes. One of them gave him a little wave.
Under any other circumstances, Brian might have
waved back. But after his experience with Lily, he'd
decided to take a little break from the opposite sex.

Meeting Lily Gallagher had thrown his brain completely out of whack. He'd never once lost control the
way he had with her. Sure, he'd seduced a fair number
of women, even had a few one-night stands, but this
had been different. Instead of feeling sated the next
morning, he felt strangely uneasy, as if he'd done
something...wrong.

But what was it? She'd wanted it as much as he had,
maybe even more. And he certainly hadn't forced the
issue. He'd given her every opportunity to call a stop
to their headlong rush into intimacy.

God, she was beautiful. And that body, it seemed to
be made for his touch. He glanced at the girls at the end
of the bar. Funny how a few nights ago he might have
found them attractive. Now they were just too...much.
Their lipstick was too dark and their hair too bleached,
their clothes too tight and their breasts too big to be
real.

Lily had been a beauty who hadn't required any im-
provements. Her hair, her skin, her slender form. Each
element had been nearly perfect in his eyes. An image
of her flashed in his head, her dress billowing around
them both, her eyes closed at the moment of her release. Brian groaned softly, then rubbed his forehead.
"Lily," he murmured.

"What?" Sean asked.

Brian gave his brother a sideways glance. "What?"

"You said 'Lily,'" Sean replied. "Lily what?"

"It's not a Lily what. It's a Lily who. She's a woman I met last night. At this fund-raiser at the Copley."

"Hmm," Sean said.

"What is that supposed to mean?"

"Nothing."

"Then just shut up!"

"Don't get pissed at me," Sean said. "I was just making conversation."

"Well, don't," Brian muttered. Silence descended on them again, both of them staring into their drinks. Then Brian cursed softly.

"Was she pretty?" Sean asked.

Brian nodded. "Yeah. And funny and smart and incredibly sexy. She was wearing this gold dress that made her look...wow. You know, I think she actually took my breath away. Did that ever happen to you?"

"Sounds like you have it bad."

"I spent one night with her."

"Tell me you didn't rescue her from some life-threatening situation," Sean said. "Or you're in big trouble."

Brian chuckled. "Naw, I didn't res—" He paused, his stomach sinking. "Oh, hell." He *had* rescued her, not from any danger, but from her boring companion! In fact, she'd even thanked him for the favor and he hadn't realized the importance of her words until now. "Yeah, I guess I did."

"Well, that's it then. Jaysus, Brian, haven't you been paying attention. Conor, Dylan, Brendan and Liam. Even Keely. It's a curse, you know. No one is immune. Not even you."

"Or you," Brian countered.

"Oh, no? I'm not crying in my club soda after a one-night stand."

"She wasn't just a one-night stand," Brian snapped.

"Did you hook up?"

"Yeah."

"Did you get her phone number? Did you make a date to see her? Are you planning to call?"

"No."

"Then it was a one-night stand."

"That makes it sound so...well, that's not what it was like. It was different. Besides, if I wanted to find her again, I could."

"Do you know where she lives?"

"No."

"You don't have her phone number. Did she tell you where she works?"

"No, but I have her name. Lily Gallagher."

"You sure that's her real name?"

"Stop talking like a P.I. If I wanted to find her, I could." In truth, Brian had been wondering about that same thing since the moment she'd dropped him off in front of the hotel. He could call the event organizers and get her address off the invitation list. He could call the limo company and find out who hired the car. Hell, he could look in the Chicago phonebook under Gallagher, if he really wanted to find her. "I don't believe in the curse," he finally said.

"Maybe you just had a close call," Sean said. "Be more careful next time. You just can't trust women."

Brian knew that Sean's feelings weren't entirely based on his own dating experiences. His distrust went back a lot further, back to their mother and her desertion of them when he and Sean were only three years old. Brian had no memories of Fiona Quinn when he was a child. They'd been told she'd left the family, then died in a car accident, a story fabricated by their bitter father. And now that Fiona Quinn was back in their lives, Brian had forgiven her past mistakes. Only Sean seemed to be carrying an old grudge.

"Ma is staying with Keely and Rafe," Brian said. "Keely called this morning and wants us all to come for a picnic on the Fourth of July. Now that she's getting her business moved up here, Fiona is thinking about moving, too. I think Keely wants to convince her that we all want her here. Are you going?"

He shook his head. "Nah, I'm busy. I'm going to be working on a case—out of town."

"What is your problem with her? You're an adult, not some pissed off little kid. She and Da had a tough time, they both made mistakes. If Da can forgive her, you should."

"I have my reasons," Sean said.

"What reasons?"

He shook his head, then reached for his Guinness and took a sip.

Brian cursed softly. "I swear, you are the most stubborn, selfish son of a bitch I've ever known."

"She cheated," Sean muttered.

"What?"

Sean kept his voice low. "Fiona. She was cheating on Da."

"How do you know that?"

"One night after the *Mighty Quinn* put into port, Conor sent me down to the pub to drag Da home. He was drunk. He was talking to some of his pals and he told them that he'd caught Fiona with another man. He said he'd kicked her out of the house and that he didn't expect her back. He didn't know I was there, that I'd heard."

"Geez, Sean, why didn't you say something?"

"What was I supposed to say? I never knew her. And the way Con and Dylan and Bren talked about her, she was like the goddamn queen of virtue and goodness and I believed that. I kept hoping she'd come home."

"What else did Da say?"

"I don't remember much of it. He was really drunk. Most of what he said didn't make sense." Sean sighed. "All those *Mighty Quinn* stories. Hell, I don't blame him. Turning over any control to a woman is dangerous."

"You've got to talk to Ma about this."

"Why? So she can make some excuse? She was supposed to love us. She was supposed to be faithful to Da. That's what marriage is all about. Till death do us part."

"People make mistakes, Sean. And marriage is difficult enough, without a husband who's away for weeks at a time and who drinks too much and who gambles his pay away."

"Are you saying she had a good excuse to cheat?"

"I'm saying you need to talk to her and get this out in the open. She wants her family back and you're part of that family."

Sean shoved his glass across the bar. "Tell Da that I'll tend bar tomorrow. I have to go."

Brian sighed as Sean strode to the door. Maybe he shouldn't have pushed so hard. But he'd been on edge all day and provoking his brother into an argument had simply been a reaction to his mood.

"I have to forget Lily Gallagher," he murmured. "I just have to forget her."

"I DON'T KNOW WHAT I'm doing here," Lily said. "Patterson hasn't explained what he needs." Grabbing a piece of paper, she sat down at her desk in the living room of her hotel suite. She slowly scribbled on the paper as she spoke to Emma Carsten, her best friend and co-worker at the agency. "We've got a meeting scheduled for Tuesday, so I guess I'll find out then."

"Why did you have to be in Boston this weekend?"

Lily drew a heart and traced over it again and again. "I don't know. I guess he wanted me to attend this benefit he was sponsoring so I could see what a good guy he is."

Emma and Lily had started work at DeLay Scoville the same month and had struggled through their first year together, calling on each other whenever they had questions. Now that they had more experience, they still discussed their clients with each other.

"Why would he come all the way to Chicago to look for a PR firm?" Emma asked. "There must be plenty of firms in Boston."

"I don't know," Lily said. "I'll have to ask him."

"He must know you're good with a scandal. Do you think he's got a scandal he wants you to fix?"

"If he does, I hope it isn't too messy or I'm going to be here for a while."

"So, what are the men like in Boston?" Emma asked. "Are they cuter than they are in Chicago? Did you meet anyone interesting at the party?"

Lily's breath caught in her throat. Brian Quinn certainly had been interesting. How many times had his image flashed in her head since last night? She'd expected to put the evening aside and get on with her work here in Boston.

But making love to Brian Quinn in the back of a limo had been the craziest, most dangerous thing she'd ever done. And rather than satisfy her desire, it only made her want more—more of his mouth and his hair and his incredible body. More of the need and excitement and shudders of ecstasy.

Lily swallowed hard. "I—I'm not here to meet men," she said. "I'm here to work."

Emma was silent for a moment. "Are you all right? You sound a little strange. Tense."

"No, I'm fine."

"Are you thinking about Daniel? This assignment was probably the best thing for you. You'll put some distance between you and him and get on with your life."

In truth, Lily hadn't thought about Daniel at all—not since the moment she'd met Brian Quinn. "I'm over him," she said. "I'm moving on. From now on, I'm not going to let myself get caught up in romantic fantasies. In fact, I'm not going to let myself fall for any man."

"I think that's a good attitude to have," Emma said. "For now."

A knock sounded on the door. "Listen, I ordered a little snack and it's here. I'll call you on Tuesday after I talk with Patterson. Make sure you water my plants. And don't let the mail pile up." They said their goodbyes and Lily hung up the phone.

She flipped on the television as she crossed the room

to the door, the sound of the eleven o'clock news filling the room. Though she'd had healthy salad and a diet soda in the hotel restaurant earlier that evening, she'd been craving sweets all evening long. She'd promised herself to get into a regular workout routine, but decided tomorrow would be a better time to start. Besides, she'd gotten a day's exercise walking around Back Bay and Beacon Hill, shopping and taking in the sights of the historic neighborhoods, learning more about the city that would be her home for the next few months.

But even with shopping to distract her, Lily's thoughts had returned again and again to the previous night. Even now, she felt her cheeks warm as she thought of what she'd done. Pausing at the door, she pressed her palms to her face. Why should she feel embarrassed? She'd decided what she wanted and she'd gone after it. Just because that involved unbridled lust and an earth-shattering orgasm didn't make it a crime.

"That's what I'll keep telling myself," she said.

Another knock sounded on the door and she pulled it open. A waiter stood outside with a tray. "Good evening, Ms. Gallagher."

"Hi," she said. "You can just put that on the table, thanks."

Lily followed him inside and signed the bill for the pie and ice cream, adding a generous tip. Richard Patterson was picking up the tab for her hotel, so why not? But as she was signing the check, a familiar voice drifted through the room. She froze, then slowly turned to face the television.

Lily's jaw dropped. There he was! Brian Quinn was sitting behind a news desk reading the news. She closed her eyes and cursed. Now she was imagining him on television, and not just in her bed or in the limo or showering in her hotel bathroom. She opened her eyes and stared at the screen, prepared to realize she'd been wrong. "Oh, my God," she murmured. "It's him."

"He's really good," the waiter said, nodding in the direction of the television.

She snapped her head around to look at him. "What?"

"That guy. Quinn. He did an investigation on the auto repair business in Boston. It was really an eye-opener. Two of the biggest dealerships in town were taking cars in for repair and they were deliberately breaking things, just so they could charge to fix them. And this Quinn just went in and stuck a microphone in their faces, daring them not to answer the tough questions."

Lily turned back to the television, her attention transfixed by the image on the screen. He really was a handsome man with his dark hair and beautiful eyes, those chiseled cheekbones and sculpted lips. A tiny shiver skittered through her as she listened to his voice. It was hard to believe this was the same man she'd been with the previous night. He'd never mentioned what he did for a living—although that had been one of their little rules.

"He usually doesn't read the news," the waiter said. "He's like an...investigative reporter. I read somewhere he's from Southie."

"Southie?"

"South Boston. Hometown boy. Working-class neighborhood."

Lily handed the check back to him. "Thanks," she murmured.

The waiter smiled and nodded. "Have a nice evening, Ms. Gallagher. Just give me a call if there's anything else I can get for you."

She didn't see the waiter leave the room. Instead, she kept her gaze fixed on the television, slowly sitting down at the table. How odd it was to be looking at him again. When he'd left her last night, she'd assumed it would be the last time she saw him. And now, here he was, in her hotel room with her.

She grabbed a fork and dug in to the piece of apple pie à la mode, her eyes still transfixed by the news broadcast. This was not supposed to happen! She wasn't supposed to feel this way. A one-night stand was supposed to last just one night!

But now she knew where to find him. He wasn't just some stranger in the night, he was a man with a job and a home and people who knew him. If she wanted, she could dial the television station right now and leave a message. And when he got that message, he'd stop by her hotel room and they'd—

Lily glanced down at the pie then methodically devoured the remainder of it in four large bites. Then she snatched up the room service menu and dialed the kitchen. "Hello. Yes, Lily Gallagher in 312. I'd like a piece of lemon meringue pie and a piece of pecan pie. And send up one of those chocolate fudge brownie sundaes, too, as well as two glasses of milk. And hurry."

She hung the phone up and went back to the television, pacing back and forth in front of it. "Stick to your guns," she muttered. "Don't imagine something that isn't there. This is all about control."

Lily groaned and sat down on the end of the sofa to wait for her food. If she was in complete control, then why did she want another night with Brian Quinn, and several more after that? And why did she feel like gobbling down an entire pie? Lily covered her face with her hands, groaning softly. "What have I done?"

3

LILY SAT IN HER OFFICE at Patterson Properties and Investments, staring out the window at the Boston skyline. She pushed up from her desk and peered down on the streets in the financial district, watching the traffic crawl along. Though Boston was beautiful, it wasn't Chicago. Lily sighed. She'd only been in town for only three days and she was already homesick.

After her breakup with Daniel, she'd decided to make some big changes in her life. She'd stumbled upon an old house for sale in the Wicker Park neighborhood of Chicago and without really thinking about it, put in an offer. The act of purchasing a home had been her first step toward independence. From the time she'd left college, Lily had always rented, believing that her perfect mate would come along, they'd get married and buy a house together.

But now, she had a mortgage payment all her own and a house in need of a new roof. A promotion at work and a big raise would go a long way toward paying the bills. If she did a good job for Richard Patterson, Don DeLay would have to see her value to the firm.

The house in Chicago hadn't been the only change. Her mind flashed back to Brian Quinn. Her little one-night stand had been part of the plan, too—a part that she was fast growing to regret.

Lily turned away from the window. Why couldn't she put Brian Quinn out of her mind? Yes, the sex had been good...all right, great. Incredible even. But she had to believe that part of the excitement came from the spontaneity of the moment. Making love to him in the back of the limo had been dangerous and wicked, completely out of character for her.

After it had happened, she been pleased with the results. It had been everything she'd needed—at that moment. And she'd expected to relive the moments over and over again in her head, the memories of the passion so strong. But she'd never expected this nagging temptation, this need to see him again.

A knock sounded on her office door and Lily jumped, then calmed herself. She'd been so edgy! Was this a side effect of unbridled lust? "Yes?"

Marie, the administrative assistant assigned to her, poked her head inside. "Mr. Patterson will see you now, Ms. Gallagher. In his office."

"Thanks, Marie." She smoothed her skirt and tucked her notepad under her arm, then walked out of her office and down the hall to the elevator. When she stepped inside, she leaned back and fixed her gaze on the numbers above the door. This was exactly how an ordinary woman turned into a brazen hussy, she mused. All she could think about was sex, sex, sex. Had there been an attractive single man in the elevator, who knows what might have happened?

"I need a hobby," she said. "Something to distract my mind. Pottery or kick-boxing. Maybe I could take singing lessons. I've always wanted to learn how to sing." She paused and glanced up at the security camera mounted in the corner of the elevator. "And maybe I should stop talking to myself now."

The elevator doors opened and Lily hurried out, making her way through the executive suites to the end of the hall. Richard Patterson's secretary stood as she approached. "Hello, Miss Gallagher. Is there anything I can bring you?"

"Coffee would be nice, Mrs. Wilburn," Lily said. "Cream and one sugar." She rapped on the door, then opened it and walked inside.

Richard Patterson nodded at her from behind a massive desk that was scrupulously organized. He pointed to a guest chair. "Good morning, Lily. I assume Mrs. Wilburn got you situated yesterday."

"She did. I have an office, an assistant and I met with your key people." Lily paused. "It looks like your public relations department has done a terrific job for you. But I still don't know what I'm doing here. You already have highly qualified people to do your PR. Why do you need me?"

He leaned back in his leather chair, bracing his elbows on the arms and steepling his fingers in front of his face. "There's a situation developing that may cause a bit of a crisis and I need someone experienced to handle it when it does. Someone from the outside, someone objective, to steer us through."

Lily studied his tense expression. "What kind of situation?"

"I'm working on a development project on the waterfront."

"The Wellston project," Lily said.

Patterson nodded. "As you know, getting a real estate project off the ground, especially one of this magnitude, can be almost impossible. There are layers and layers of red tape to cut through and if I can't cut through it all in an expeditious manner, I lose my investors and the project falls apart. The Wellston project was about to implode when I found a way to make it go."

"And?" Lily asked, a sick feeling growing in her stomach. "Or maybe I shouldn't ask?"

"I think it's best if you know everything. Let me just say that whether or not we broke laws is subject to the interpretation of those laws. We had to do some things that might not have been completely ethical. There are suspicions of impropriety. And certain people in the media have been gunning for me ever since I got approval on the Minuteman Mall project. They won't consider the…nuances involved in making a deal work. If the details of this story break, my investors will pull out and I'll be ruined. Patterson Properties and Investments will go under, taking hundreds of jobs with it. I need to make sure that story doesn't come out. I saw the way you handled that bribery scandal for that developer in Chicago. Can you do the same thing for me?"

Lily groaned inwardly. She was considered an expert in crisis public relations, but it was always easier when the client hadn't broken any laws. Heck, a nice juicy sex scandal was a snap compared to the looming threat of a trial and prison time. If she had to choose between morality and legality, morality was the far easier problem to solve.

"You need to know three things," Lily said. "First, I won't break any laws for you. Second, I'm not going to lie for you. I may not be forthcoming with the truth, I may refuse to answer questions, but I won't lie."

"And third?"

"If I take this job, you'll take my advice. You'll do *exactly* as I advise. I'm not sure if I can avert disaster here, but I can certainly try my best to make your problems seem less...newsworthy."

"All right." He picked up a file folder from the center of his desk. "The first guy I need you to neutralize is Brian Quinn."

Lily's breath froze in her throat and her eyes went wide. "Brian Quinn? How do you know about him?"

"He's been nosing into my business affairs for the past six months. He's a hotshot investigative reporter at WBTN and he thinks if he can dig up dirt on me, he'll have a story worth six or seven rating points. The guy needs to be stopped. Do whatever it takes."

Lily snatched up the file folder and looked at it, flipping through a lengthy report. "What is this?"

"I hired a private investigator to tail him. There's plenty there. He has quite a reputation with the ladies, a different girl every week. His father owns some seedy pub down in Southie. We might be able to use that as leverage, maybe cause some problem with the old man's permits. His father was also arrested a year ago for murder."

"Oh, my God," Lily said. "Murder?"

"It's all in the file. The P.I. has been trailing him for about a month now. I should have another report in a few days. The investigator is digging into his past. I've had my people pull news clips for you and tapes of his reports. Get to know him, I want strategies on how to counteract his interference. You don't need to okay anything with me. Just get the job done." With that, Patterson stood, effectively ending their meeting.

Lily jumped up from her chair and nodded to him. "I'll get right on it."

She walked out as Mrs. Wilburn was coming in with her cup of coffee. Lily shrugged apologetically, but continued her retreat. When she reached the safety of her office, she closed the door behind her and took a deep breath, her head spinning and her stomach in knots.

The report inside the file folder was ten pages long and Lily quickly skimmed the text, stunned at how detailed it was. She flipped back to the first page and noted the date. It was dated a couple of weeks before her encounter with Brian Quinn in the back of the limo.

She groaned softly. But the private investigator had continued to tail Brian Quinn after this report. Right now, he could be typing up a report about their tryst! It wouldn't be difficult to find out her name. It had been on the invitation list. Lily frowned. But Brian's hadn't. He claimed he'd crashed the party. Considering the situation now, Lily couldn't help but think that he'd come there deliberately to collect more dirt on Richard Patterson.

"He has no shame."

Another notion suddenly occurred to her. Could he have known who she was before he approached her at the fund-raiser? Lily shook her head. He'd have to have been the best investigative reporter on the planet to know she'd be coming into town, much less know her reason for her being there.

Lily grabbed the phone book and flipped through it. There were too many unanswered questions that were certain to plague her. When she found the number and address for WBTN, she scribbled it on a scrap of paper. Then she drew a deep breath. She'd have to handle this very carefully. She couldn't just walk into the station and confront him. Instead, there had to be some way to get him on neutral turf.

"I could just call him and ask him for a date," she murmured, picking up the phone. But that would be admitting she'd felt more for him than just a passing desire. "No, there has to be another way."

Lily had strategized plans for multimillion-dollar clients. She should be able to figure out how to approach Brian Quinn. But why was she really interested in seeing him? To figure out what he knew about Richard Patterson's business dealings? Or maybe to convince him to back off the story? She cursed softly. Maybe her need to see him was less professional and more personal.

A idea struck her and she grabbed up the phone and punched in the station's number. The receptionist answered the phone and Lily gathered her resolve. "I'd like to speak to Brian Quinn," she said, trying to disguise her voice, make it sound deeper, older.

"One moment, I'll put you through."

Another phone rang and a woman answered. "Newsroom," she said.

"Brian Quinn, please," Lily said.

"May I ask what this is regarding?"

"I want to talk to him about Richard Patterson," she said. "I have some information he might be interested in." The phone clicked and the audio for a soap opera came on. A few seconds later, the line clicked again.

"Brian Quinn."

Lily's heart hammered in her chest at the sound of his voice, so deep and smooth. "Mr. Quinn?"

"Who is this?"

"My name isn't important. I have some information I'd like to share with you...about Richard Patterson. Is there someplace we can meet?"

The line was silent for a moment. "All right. There's a place in Southie, a pub. Quinn's Pub."

"Quinn's?"

"My father owns it. We'll be able to talk there. Trust me. How will I know you?"

"I'll know you. Three p.m. today," Lily said. "Be there." She quickly hung up the phone and then drew a deep breath, her head still spinning. His father's pub was still on his turf, but if she had protested too much, he might have gotten suspicious. Quinn's Pub was as good a place as any to confront him.

"So what am I going to say?" Lily rubbed her forehead, trying to banish the confusion that muddled her brain. Whatever she said, she'd need to make sure that he had no doubt about where she stood. She was not going to jump in the back seat of the nearest car and repeat what they'd shared that night in the limo. She'd be polite and warn him to stay away from Richard Patterson. She'd ignore his sexy smile and his incredible body and the way he looked at her, as if he wanted nothing more than to rip all her clothes off and ravish her.

"I can do this," Lily muttered. "This isn't just a job— it's an adventure."

BRIAN PARKED HIS CAR in front of Quinn's Pub five minutes before three. He jumped out, then looked up and down the street, wondering if his contact would be waiting outside. He knew it was a woman, but that was all he knew.

As an investigative reporter, he'd spent countless hours tracking down people who might be willing to spill their guts, convincing ex-secretaries and nosy neighbors and even relatives to turn on those he felt were guilty of some type of misbehavior. He suspected that this woman was probably an employee, or if he was lucky, an ex-lover of Patterson's, someone who might break this story wide open.

He took the steps two at a time and pulled the front door open. Thankfully, the bar was nearly empty. A few of the regulars sat at one end, playing cards with Seamus. And a couple sat at one of the tables, eating lunch. Though the pub had been busy since the Roamer's listing, three o' clock was long after the lunch rush and well before happy hour.

"Hey, Da," Brian called. Seamus tossed his cards down, but Brian held out his hand. "I'll get my own drink."

He stepped around the end of the bar and grabbed a bottled water from the refrigerator, then sat down on a stool to wait. Hell, he wasn't even sure she'd show up. A large percentage of his contacts ended up backing out at the last minute, worried that their comments might somehow put their safety at risk. But Brian had learned to be pragmatic and patient about getting a story. A good story, one worth reporting, usually revealed itself in its own good time.

The door opened behind him and Brian turned around, only to find his brother Sean strolling in. Sean nodded at him and took the stool beside him. "Hey, Brian," his brother murmured.

"Sean," Brian replied.

"I was hoping I'd find you here." Sean reached into his jacket pocket and retrieved a piece of paper from his pocket. He slid it across the bar to Brian. "There you go."

"What's this?"

"Lily Gallagher. She's staying at the Eliot on Commonwealth. Room 312."

Brian gasped, then shoved the paper back at his brother. "I didn't ask you to find her."

"You didn't have to. Since you're going to be marrying her, I figured you'd want to know where she was."

Brian stood. "Goddamn it, I'm not going to marry her!"

Sean shrugged. "So you say. I think it's pretty much a done deal." He retrieved the paper, but at the last minute, Brian snatched it from his fingers. His brother grinned. "I rest my case."

"Did you come here for a reason or were you simply interested in tormenting me?"

Sean reached in another jacket pocket and produced a sheaf of papers. "These are the names of some people who have left the employ of Richard Patterson over the past year. You asked me to get these for you a few weeks ago, remember?"

Brian irritation faded as he stared at the long list. "Wow, I didn't think you'd be able to get something so quick."

"There are seventeen names. Secretaries, middle management and one guy from the financial office."

"Thanks, bro. I owe you."

Sean pushed away from the bar. "I'll send you a bill," he said, a crooked smile curving his lips. "I have to go. See ya later."

Brian watched as his brother walked to the door. Sean pulled it open, then stopped and danced back and forth with another patron who was trying to get inside. Finally, Sean stepped aside and the woman came in, turning to stare at Sean with her mouth agape.

Brian slowly stood. "Lily?" He blinked, certain that he was simply engaged in some strange fantasy. But it was her. Lily Gallagher was in Quinn's Pub. What the hell was she doing here? Had he mentioned the place to her? Had she come looking for him?

He sighed. God, she looked pretty. Her auburn hair was pulled back and twisted at the nape of her neck. She wore a conservative business suit that served to hide all her assets, but she still took his breath away the same way she had the first time he'd seen her in her gold gown and sexy little shoes.

Her mouth snapped shut as she saw him, then she frowned and glanced back at the door.

Brian slowly approached her. "My twin brother, Sean," he explained. "People say we look alike, but I don't see it. What are you doing here? I didn't expect to see you again."

She crossed her arms in front of her, her eyes darting everywhere but to his face. "We had an appointment. At three p.m.?"

Brian frowned. "You're my contact? How can that be?"

"I work for Richard Patterson," she said, her voice calm, almost cold.

He gasped. "Are you kidding me?"

"I'm a public relations consultant. And he hired me to protect him from people like you."

He couldn't help but laugh. She made him sound like some kind of criminal. "People like me?"

"Reporters." She said the word as if it caused a vile taste in her mouth. "So just stay away, or you'll be sorry." Then she cursed softly and walked away. But just as she reached the door, she turned around and stalked back to him, her impassive expression now suffused with anger. "You know this is all your fault. If you wouldn't have suggested those silly rules when we met, then none of this would have happened. I would have known who you were and you would have known who I was and we could have avoided...well, we'd never have taken that little tour of Boston."

"You work for Richard Patterson," Brian said. "So what. The only thing that could make me regret what happened in the limo was if you announced that you were Richard Patterson's wife."

Lily shook her head. "I have to go. I just wanted you to know that I'm going to do everything in my power to protect his interests. It's my job and I'm very, *very* good at my job." She turned on her heel and started back to the door, but Brian wasn't about to let her walk out.

He caught up with her in a few short steps and grabbed her hand. The moment he touched her, he realized that she wasn't nearly as tough as she acted. Her voice caught in her throat and she stumbled slightly. "Wait a second," he murmured. "You can't just leave like that. We have a few more things to talk about."

Lily swallowed hard, then twisted out of his grasp. "We—we have nothing more to talk about. You know where I stand and I know where you stand. That's all that needs to be—" His gaze caught hers and for a moment, it seemed as if she forgot what she wanted to say. "Said," she finished in a weak voice.

"You're acting like there's nothing more between us, Lily. And you know that's not true."

She gnawed on her lower lip. "There's nothing between us," she said. She pulled the door open and stumbled down the steps. For a second, he considered letting her go. But Brian wasn't willing to concede that this might be the last time he ever saw her. He jogged over to her, stepping in front of her to prevent her escape.

"You just used me for sex and then tossed me aside," he said, walking backward. "I guess I didn't realize how coldhearted you really were." That caused her to stop short.

"I didn't use—" She snapped her mouth shut, but her emotions were all there in her eyes—anger, frustration, a good measure of doubt and insecurity. And hidden behind it all, an undeniable attraction.

He reached out to take her hand. "I know you felt something, Lily," he said, softening his tone. "Remember, I was there. It may have started out as just sex, but it didn't end that way, did it?" It felt good to touch her again, Brian mused. In truth, it was all he could do not to yank her into his arms and kiss away this stupid argument.

"Don't make this about that night," Lily warned, her voice cracking slightly. "That was a mistake and this is a completely separate issue."

"Well then, let's agree that we're both going to do our jobs to the best of our abilities. I'm going to go after Patterson hard and you're going to try to stop me. That's fine with me. May the best person win."

"It was sex," Lily murmured.

"You keep believing that, Lily. You believe that you were just using me, that you just wanted to take your pleasure and walk away. But you won't convince me. I was there. I saw you, I *felt* you. And right now, you're looking at me and wondering just what you'd have to do to make it all happen again."

"Stop it!" she cried. Lily glanced around. "I'm leaving now and I don't ever want to see you again."

She started toward the street, but in her anger she wasn't watching for traffic. Brian caught her just as she stepped off the curb. He yanked her back as a car sped by. "Lily, stop. You can't just run out in the—"

"Let go of me!"

Frustrated, he grabbed her other arm and yanked her into his embrace, then kissed her, long and hard. At first, she refused to yield, but then he softened his assault and she slowly went limp in his arms. A tiny moan slipped from her throat and her hands moved from his chest to his neck. Brian had forgotten just how intoxicating she tasted, how when their tongues touched, he seemed to lose the ability to think.

He'd kissed a lot of women and had considered himself pretty good at it. But with Lily, the experience was something more than just the first step in seduction. It was like a silent communication, a chance to share some brief intimacy that he hadn't ever shared with another woman.

When he had kissed her as thoroughly as he possibly

could, Brian stepped away and waited for her reaction. He didn't have to wait long. Desire flooded her expression and she fixed her gaze on his mouth, her lips slightly swollen and her ivory complexion flushed. "You can kiss me all day and it's not going to change my mind."

Brian chuckled. Her words didn't seem like a threat, but more like an invitation. "Now there's an idea. Would you like to get started right here or should we find some place a little more comfortable?"

Her brow rose and annoyance replaced desire. "I think you must be the most self-centered, egotistical man I've ever met."

Brian chuckled. "But I know how to kiss you like no one's ever kissed you before."

Her jaw tensed and with a low growl, she walked away from him, crossing the street to a waiting cab. Brian watched as she drove off, then shook his head and started toward his car. After he'd left her that night in the limo, he'd been sure he'd never see her again. And now, Brian knew it was only a matter of time before they'd cross paths once more. And when they did, it promised to be an interesting experience.

LILY TOSSED her briefcase on the sofa and kicked off her shoes. It was nearly seven and she'd spent a long day at the office going over all of Richard Patterson's press clippings for the past year. She'd looked at videotape of newscasts and flipped through business magazines until she had a good sense of which members of the press were friends and which were enemies. She'd met with his legal team to get their take on the situation.

And she mapped out a strategy to contain any scandal that might come to light.

There was no doubt in her mind that Brian Quinn would come at them hard. From what she could see, he was relentless in the pursuit of a juicy story. She couldn't really fault him for that. From the moment she'd begun her career in public relations, she'd been just as focused on her own goals.

But she'd never really doubted herself. And now, she wondered if maybe she'd stepped into the deep end without a life jacket. If Richard Patterson's business dealings were on the dark side of shady, it would be difficult to make the scandal go away. And an unhappy client was sometimes worse than an unsatisfactory outcome. Added to that, she was also forced to deal with a single-minded reporter who had the capacity to kiss her senseless.

"Just do the job," she murmured, flopping down on the sofa. She reached back and undid the pins from her hair, pulling it free from the confining knot.

Brian had already broadcast one report on the protests against the Wellston waterfront project and it was clear that he had Patterson in his sights. Compared to the community groups who had opposed the project, Quinn was more dangerous. He could reach thousands of viewers a night and affect the decisions of people in power.

Lily felt almost impotent in dealing with him. She had shown him her weaknesses that afternoon in the pub and if he was any type of reporter, he'd exploit them at the first possible opportunity. She groaned softly and rubbed her temples, trying to drive thoughts of work from her head. With this job, more than any other, she needed to leave it at the office or she'd be a basket case by the time she left town.

But that would be easier said than done. Without a social life in Boston, she had no choice but to spend her days *and* her evenings thinking about work. She'd already broken her own promise to start a workout routine. Lily reached for the box of Milk Duds she'd bought from the vending machine and popped a few in her mouth. Tomorrow was soon enough to get started.

A knock sounded on her door and Lily scrambled off the bed. She hadn't called for dinner yet, but maybe it was the maid with the chocolates for the pillow! Lily yanked the door open, only to find Brian Quinn standing on the other side. He held up a bouquet of flowers, a wide grin on his handsome face. Her heart did a little flip and had she been able to reach inside her chest and slap it, she would have.

"Hi there," he said, his gaze skimming her face and coming to rest on her lips.

Lily groaned and made to close the door, but he gently pushed it open. This was the last thing she needed tonight. "What are you doing here? How did you find out where I was staying?"

"I'm Brian Quinn, investigative reporter," he teased. "I have sources everywhere."

"I don't want to talk to you. We don't have anything to say to each other."

"All right, we won't talk. Let's go."

"Go where?"

"To dinner. You're new to Boston. I know all the best places to eat *and* I can get in without reservations. I'm inviting you to accompany me to dinner. You don't have to say a word. We won't talk about work, we won't talk about sex, we won't talk at all, we'll just eat."

"I'm not going on a date with you!" Lily cried.

"Did I say this was a date?"

She sent him a sarcastic smile. "Haven't I explained this already? Are you Brian Quinn, reporter, or Brian Quinn, hearing-impaired jackass?"

"I don't think the fact that we're working on opposite sides of an issue should have any bearing on whether we eat together. I can separate my social life from my professional life. Can't you?"

"Of course I can," Lily lied, walking into the room. "I just don't want to at the present moment."

"You haven't even tried," he said, following her inside. "I'm a very charming man and a brilliant conversationalist. I'm also witty and handsome. And modest. Come out to dinner with me and if you're having a horrible time, then you can go home. You have to eat, don't you?"

"I'm tired. I was going to order room service."

Brian shrugged and sat down on the edge of the sofa, stretching his arms across the back and crossing his leg over his knee. "That sounds good, too. Can I see the menu?"

Lily hitched her hands on her hips. "If you don't get off that sofa and out of my room, I'm going to call security and have them throw you out. But first, I'm going to call the media so they'll have cameras ready to witness your graceful exit. And I might just also let slip about your fondness for whips, leather underwear and four-inch heels. Don't you just hate it when the news reporters end up making the news?"

Brian chuckled. "You've been in town for three days. You don't have any juice yet with the local media. No one knows you. They won't show up. So where's the menu? I could go for a burger. How about you?"

God, she hated that he was always one step ahead of her! If this was any indication of how she was going to control the situation, she might as well catch the next plane back to Chicago. She sighed and raked her hand through her hair. "You're not going to leave, are you?"

"Nope."

Lily walked over to the desk and grabbed the room service menu, then threw it at him. To her frustration, he caught it with one hand. "So, how was your day?" he asked as he perused the menu.

"Do you really expect me to answer that?"

"I was just making polite conversation."

Lily strolled over to the easy chair. "I'll tell you, honestly. It was busy. I spent the day looking at media coverage of Richard Patterson. I must say, you haven't been kind. Your report on his Minuteman project was very unflattering. And you didn't check your facts very well." Lily folded her hands on her lap and stared at him, trying to convince herself that he wasn't as handsome as she remembered. "You know, you still owe me two questions."

Brian frowned. "That was Saturday night."

"I don't recall there being a time limit, do you? No? Question number four. What do you have on Richard Patterson?"

"I'm not going to tell you that," Brian said.

"You have to. Total honesty, remember? That was the deal." Lily couldn't help but smile. Now she finally had the upper hand, at least for the moment.

He sat silently and considered the question. "Let's order dinner first and then I'll tell you everything. What will you have?"

Grudgingly, Lily grabbed the menu. "A small salad with vinaigrette dressing, steamed vegetables, and a glass of red wine. By the way, Richard Patterson is paying for this room and the meal. I don't know if you have any ethical problems with that but I just thought I'd warn you. You're eating on his dime."

"I'll buy dinner." He picked up the phone and dialed room service. "Yes. We'll have two New York strip steaks, baked potato, crème brûlée for dessert and a bottle of your best champagne. Oh, and add a shrimp cocktail and some oysters to that as well." Then he proceeded to offer his credit card number.

"I wanted a salad," Lily said.

"Oops," Brian said. "Since I'm paying, you'll have to eat what I ordered."

Lily shook her head. "You are really a pain."

He hung up the phone. "You haven't seen anything yet. Now, you wanted to know what I've got. I know that Richard Patterson has had to make some sleazy deals to get the Wellston project off the ground. Bribes, influence peddling, probably a few illegal campaign contributions. That waterfront project has been tangled in legalities for years. Three different developers have owned the property and they couldn't make it work, yet he suddenly can? Something smells bad here."

"What proof do you have?"

"None...yet. But it's out there. I just have to find it. Now, let's talk about something else."

"Next question," Lily said. "What do you—"

"No," he interrupted. "I told you what I had on Patterson and I told you what proof I had. Two questions, two answers."

Frustrated, Lily stood up and walked to the bedroom. "I'm going to change. When I come back, I'd be elated if I found you gone."

Lily stepped into the dark bedroom and closed the French doors behind her, leaning back against them for a moment to catch her breath. She couldn't deny the fact that she'd been thrilled to see Brian. Even though he drove her to distraction, there was something about him that she found completely disarming. That nearly-black hair that fell into his eyes every now and then. And those odd greenish-gold eyes. Oh, and that body. He definitely had the most incredible body.

Had the notion not been completely ridiculous, she might have considered prolonging their "relationship" for a while longer. With a soft moan, Lily crossed the room to the dresser and pulled out a T-shirt and jeans. She slipped out of her jacket and skirt, then walked into the bathroom, unbuttoning her blouse along the way.

When she got to the bathroom, she turned on the water at the sink and scrubbed her face clean. Then she pulled off her panty hose and kicked them aside before walking back into the bedroom.

"I'd forgotten how beautiful you were."

Lily's breath caught in her throat as she looked up to find Brian standing in the doorway, the light from the sitting room streaming in behind him. They stared at each other for a long time, Lily's heartbeat measuring out the seconds. She was afraid to move, afraid to breathe, afraid that if she even acknowledged his presence she might spontaneously combust.

Then, a tiny sigh slipped from her throat and it was like a quiet surrender. At the same moment, they moved to each other, Brian gathering her in his arms, Lily collapsing against his body, their mouths meeting in a desperate kiss. His hands frantically skimmed over her body, beneath her silk shirt, over her lacy bra, down her back and around her hips.

Though Lily knew she should fight the desire, she couldn't summon the energy. She loved the way his mouth tasted and the way his hands felt on her skin. Blood pounded in her veins, awakening every nerve in her body until the simplest caress sent waves of sensation racing through her.

He grabbed her backside and lifted her up, wrapping her legs around his waist. Their mouths still locked, he moved to the bed, but stopped halfway there to press her against the wall. His hips ground against hers and she arched toward him, remembering how it felt to have him inside of her, the wild sensations created by their shared release.

Lily tore at his shirt, aching to feel his body beneath her fingers and he did the same, shoving her shirt off her shoulders and exploring the skin beneath with his mouth.

"God, Lily, what are you doing to me?" he murmured.

And then, just as suddenly as it started, it stopped. His breath came in deep gasps and he pressed his lips to her shoulder, nuzzling her shirt aside. "Are we going to do this again?"

She grabbed his face and kissed him again. "Yes," she murmured.

"Yes," he repeated, savaging her mouth with his tongue. Then he drew back. "No."

"No?"

He slowly lowered her to the floor, then fussed with the front of her blouse, adjusting it until he could button the top two buttons. "Even though I'd love nothing more than to spend an evening in bed with you, I think we need to exercise some restraint." He chuckled softly. "I can't believe I'm saying this. I'm just a heartbeat away from tearing that blouse off of you."

Brian stepped back, then lowered his hands to his sides. "I have to go. I'll...see you. We'll have dinner sometime. In a restaurant. A well-lit, very crowded restaurant." He gave her a quick kiss, then straightened his clothes as he walked out of the bedroom.

Lily heard the door to her suite close and she leaned back against the wall and willed her heart to slow to a reasonable pace. Raising her fingers to her lips, she sighed softly. She could still taste him, smell him and feel his body against hers. It hadn't been a fantasy or a dream, he'd been here and they'd nearly lost themselves in each other again.

She wasn't sure how long she stood there, waiting for her breathing to return to normal. Her eyes were closed when she heard a knock at the door. For a moment, she considered not answering, certain that if she let him into the room again, they'd end up in bed. But then, Lily realized that she wanted him—beyond all reason.

She hurried to the door and pulled it open, but it was only the room service waiter who stood outside. "Good evening, Ms. Gallagher. I have your dinner."

Lily stepped aside as he pushed the cart into the

room. By the time she got a hold of her emotions, he'd laid the dinner out on the table and was making his way toward the door. When she was alone again, she wandered to the table and picked up the crème brûlée, cracking through the hard sugar topping to the custard beneath.

This was exactly what had gotten her in trouble in the first place. Eating dessert before trying the appetizers and main course. With Brian, she'd been focused on instant gratification, certain that sex was all she really wanted. But now, she wondered what might have happened if she'd done things in the proper order, calling on a bit of willpower.

She took a bite of the crème brûlée and let the silken custard melt on her tongue. "This is better than sex," she murmured. "I just need to eat more dessert. Then all these crazy feelings will disappear."

4

"I NEED the camera goddess!"

Brian grabbed his jacket and slipped it on, then searched his desk for a tie. He liked to look respectable when he appeared on-air, but sometimes news happened, whether he was dressed for it or not.

"Taneesha!" he shouted, striding through the newsroom. He poked his head into the editing suite and found her sitting at the control board with one of the news editors.

"Come on," he said. "We have to go."

Taneesha glanced up. "I need to get this offline editing done by noon. They want this piece for the six o'clock news."

"This is more important," he said. "Jerry can finish that for you, can't you, Jerry?"

The tape editor nodded. Taneesha got up and followed Brian through the door. "What's up?"

"A judge just issued an injunction on Patterson's waterfront project. He claims there are some irregularities with the financing that need to be explored. Dave is going to get me a transcript of the court report. We have to go ask Patterson what he thinks. Catch his reaction on camera."

"Quinn, we don't have a story here. You've got the news director and the station manager telling you to back off. If we go sticking a camera in Patterson's face, it's going to come back and bite both of us in the butt. He'll file harassment charges if you're not careful."

"I'll take full responsibility," he said. "Bob's got the van parked in back. I need you to get me a good shot. We're building our case here. Persistence will pay off."

Taneesha grudgingly agreed, picking up her pace as they headed to the station's parking lot. As Bob promised, he was waiting with the engine running. Taneesha was the best cameraperson at the station and in Brian's opinion, Bob was the best driver. He wove in and out of lunch hour traffic, easily making it from the station to the financial district in less than ten minutes. He pulled up in a No Parking zone in front of Patterson's office building.

"So, how are we going to do this?"

"Patterson has a meeting this afternoon with his investors at his club. His driver is scheduled to pick him up here in a few minutes." Brian pointed to a Lincoln Town Car parked in front of them. "That's his car. So I figure, he's coming this way."

"How did you know he had a meeting?" Taneesha asked, grabbing up the camera. She checked the battery pack, then balanced it on her shoulder.

"The guy who owns the car company that Patterson uses is an old high school buddy. We once stole a television together."

Taneesha gasped. "You stole a television?"

"It was just sitting there on the back of the delivery truck. I had very bad impulse control when I was young."

"And I can see you haven't changed much," she muttered.

Brian stared out the window at the front entrance to

the office tower. "He'll see the van when he comes out. If he turns and runs, I want to get that on tape, too. The fact that he won't want to talk to the media will make even a bigger statement." He paused as the doors came open. "Here he is," Brian murmured. "Get ready."

But just as Brian was ready to hop out of the van, he noticed a figure exiting the building right behind Patterson. "Lily," he murmured, his hand frozen on the door handle. For a long moment, he didn't move, her presence causing him to rethink his actions.

"Quinn!" Taneesha whispered.

"What?"

"If you don't go now, I'm not going to get a chance to focus. Go, go!" Taneesha urged.

Brian yanked the van door open and hopped out, grabbing his microphone and switching it on. Taneesha followed with the camera. "Okay," she said. "I've got him. Go ahead."

Brian kept his eyes fixed on Patterson, afraid to even glance at Lily. She was the perfect distraction, dressed in her tidy little business suit, her hair pulled back into a prissy knot. He imagined removing the hairpins one by one and letting her—geez, he had to remember his purpose here! "Mr. Patterson," he called. "Judge Ramirez has issued an injunction to stop the waterfront project. Do you have a comment?"

"No comment," Patterson growled, staring directly into the camera.

"He claims that an investigation by an independent panel found some financial irregularities. Would you like to explain what he found?"

"No comment," he said, picking up his pace.

"How much money did your company contribute to

Senator Jerry Morgan's last campaign? Was that money given in return for favors?"

Patterson quickly slipped into the car and slammed the door.

"Mr. Patterson is late for a meeting, but I'll be happy to answer any questions you might have."

Brian turned back to Lily. She smiled at him, but he could see the anger glittering in her eyes.

"Mr. Patterson's contributions to Jerry Morgan's campaign are a matter of public record. As for the injunction, we're confident that once given the chance, we'll be able to answer the court's questions to their satisfaction. The waterfront project will provide hundreds of jobs for Boston residents and Mr. Patterson believes that this will be of great help to the citizens of this city in these tough economic times. If you have any further questions, please feel free to call me."

"And what is your name?" Brian asked.

"Lily Gallagher. That's G-A-L-L-A-G-H-E-R. Lily with one 'L'. Got that?" Her eyebrow arched in a subtle challenge.

Brian grinned. "Yeah, I got that."

"Good. I wouldn't want you to make any mistakes." She leveled a disdainful gaze at him, then turned on her heel and started back inside.

Brian watched her retreat, his gaze dropping to the enticing sway of her hips and the shift of her backside beneath the formfitting skirt.

"Brrrr," Taneesha said. "I'm feeling a little chilly." She started toward the truck. "This was a waste of time. A comment by the ice queen and that's about it."

The ice queen? That description couldn't be further from the truth, Brian mused. But Brian wasn't about to tell Taneesha that Lily had the capacity to generate more "heat" than any women he'd ever touched. Just the scent of her hair or the sound of her voice was enough to make him ache for her.

He handed the microphone to Taneesha. "We're through here," he murmured. "I'll meet you back at the station." He jogged to the entrance.

"Where are you going?" Taneesha shouted.

"I've got a few follow-up questions," he said, waving. Brian caught up to her at the elevator, smoothly stepping between her and the doors. "Hi, Lily," he murmured. "It is Lily, right? Lily G-A-L-L-A-G-H-E-R?"

Lily crossed her arms over her breasts and sent him an uneasy look. "I—I don't have anything more to say to you."

"I told you I wasn't going to back off," Brian said. "People are starting to talk about Patterson. It's only a matter of time, Lily. You can't save this guy."

"I'm going to do my job," she said, straightening her spine.

"And I'm going to do mine," he countered. "Have you had lunch yet? I know this great seafood place just a few blocks from here." He grabbed her hand, weaving his fingers through hers. "Come on. You'll love it."

Lily stared down at their tangled fingers, then suddenly yanked her hand from his. "No! I'm not going to lunch with you. I'm not going anywhere with you. We will not be seeing each other outside of my capacity as Richard Patterson's media spokesperson. And you can quote me on that."

She punched the button on the elevator over and over again, as if she were frantic to get away from him, but the doors still didn't open. A few seconds later, a maintenance man carrying a toolbox walked up beside them. "That elevator is out," he mumbled. "Some idiot hit the stop button and now it won't start. You can wait for the other one or use the west elevators."

Lily started toward the stairs and Brian had no choice but to follow. "You know Patterson is ass deep in alligators, here," he shouted. "If I don't expose him, some other news reporter will. At least with me, you know I'll get the facts straight."

"I was hired to do a job and I'm going to do it," Lily said, shoving open the stairwell door.

Brian jogged after her. "Don't you have any ethical qualms about this?"

She stopped at the first landing and turned to face him. "What does this come down to? A little piece of property with a view of the water? We're not talking about war or disease or famine here. We're talking about a shopping mall and a few restaurants and some condos. I think you're the one who needs a little perspective. Why don't you go investigate some drug dealer or murderer?"

Brian stared at her for a long moment. He was sick of talking business. There were so many more pleasant things to talk about when he was with Lily. "You're thinking about kissing me right now, aren't you," he said.

Lily gasped. "Wh—what?"

"You heard me." He glanced around the stairwell and frowned. "What the hell are we doing in here? Patterson's office is on the twentieth floor."

"I'm in shape," she said. She jogged up another flight of stairs and Brian groaned softly. Though he worked out, twenty floors was a long way up. After chasing her that far, he might not have the energy to kiss her. With a low curse, he slipped out of his jacket, dropped it on the floor and started up after her.

"You can admit it, you know," he called, his voice echoing through the stairwell.

"Admit what?"

"You like me. I'm not afraid to admit that I like you."

She stopped on the next landing, then slowly turned. Step by step, she descended. But when she was just above him, her heel caught on the edge of the step and she lurched forward. He reached out and caught her in his arms, slowly letting her body come to rest against his. Brian smiled and bent forward, waiting for her to surrender to a kiss. Five seconds later, he was still waiting.

A weak smile twitched at her lips. "Now who's thinking about kissing who?" she murmured.

"Whom," he corrected.

She pushed away from him, then smoothed her hands over the front of her suit. "This is war," she said. "And I'm not about to cozy up to the enemy."

"It doesn't have to be war," he said, leaning forward and brushing his lips over hers. He waited for a moment, sure she'd retreat up the stairs. But when she didn't, he tried again, this time testing her lips with his tongue. Lily hesitated but then opened for him, a tiny sigh slipping from her as she did.

Brian picked her up, his arms wrapped around her waist, and set her down beside him, then captured her face in his hands. Their kiss turned more intense as Lily ran her hands over his chest. Kissing Lily was always an adventure. He was never quite sure how she'd respond, but when she reciprocated, he found himself instantly caught in a vortex of desire.

Her body was soft beneath the conservative clothes. He slipped his hands under her jacket and circled her waist, then yanked her closer, her hips tight against his. Clothes were a barrier to his need and he tugged at her blouse at the same time she fumbled with the buttons of his shirt.

Why did he want her so much? He'd had other women but Lily was different. Whenever he was near her—and even when he wasn't—he needed to touch her, to kiss her…to reassure himself that she was really there. Was this all about the chase? Brian had been known to be relentless in his pursuit of the opposite sex, only to grow bored once he'd made the conquest.

His thoughts jumped back to the first night they'd spent together, to that moment when he'd "saved" her from a boring evening with a boring man. Maybe Sean had been right to warn him. His brothers had fallen victim to the Quinn curse. But Brian thought that if he just didn't believe in it then he wouldn't be affected by it.

A door creaked above them and Lily froze. He slowly drew back and gazed down at her, her eyes wide. She blinked, then swore. "That is absolutely the last time I let you kiss me." Frantically, she rearranged her clothes, then hurried up the steps.

Brian didn't follow her. Instead, he leaned back against the wall and raked his fingers through his hair. Maybe he ought to heed her warnings. After all, he couldn't seem to control himself when he touched her. Considering that little problem, he might do something stupid—like fall in love. And recent history had proved that when a Quinn fell in love, there was no way out.

"WE NEED A STRATEGY," Lily said, pacing the width of the conference room. "Brian Quinn isn't going to give up."

Her mind flashed back to the kiss they'd shared in the stairwell and realized she might as well be talking about the undeniable desire between them, rather than her problems with Patterson.

Up until that kiss, Lily had maintained the delusion that she was still in control of her feelings for him. But all it had taken was a simple meeting of lips to make her realize he held some strange power over her, the power to turn her into a woman obsessed with her own lust. She just had to avoid him, that was the only solution to her problem.

"I'll just have to avoid him," Lily repeated.

She glanced around the room at Patterson's public relations staff, then forced a smile. "The injunction will be lifted within the week and we're going to schedule the ground-breaking right after that. Meanwhile, I need you all to flood the media with positive messages. We need the public to turn on Quinn. We need them to see that the waterfront project is good for Boston and that he's just stirring up trouble for his own benefit."

"But he's one of the most popular reporters in Boston," Derrick Simpson said. "His Q rating has been through the roof for a year now, especially with women."

Lily sighed. Yes, she did have a difficult job ahead of her and there was no doubt the women of Boston found him as irresistible as she did. But there had to be a way to get Brian Quinn to back off the story. Just the whiff of a scandal was enough to drive investors away. "We need to shift his focus," Lily said. "What we really need is a bigger scandal. Some public official taking a bribe or some celebrity caught sleeping with his sister-in-law."

"You can't make that happen, can you?" Margaret Kinger asked.

Lily frowned. "Shift his focus?"

"No, make a celebrity sleep with his sister-in-law."

She smiled. "I'm good, but not that good. But there should be a way to keep Brian Quinn distracted." Lily quickly evaluated her options. "We could...mislead him. Make it so he's not sure which sources to believe and which to discredit. It will be difficult for him to track down the truth that he might not have time to get the story straight."

"That's a great idea," John Kostryki said. "We can plant some false leads. And then, if he's lazy and reports them without checking his sources, we've got him. His reputation as a reporter in this town will be ruined."

Lily hesitated. She shouldn't have any qualms about hitting Brian Quinn right where it hurt—in his reputation. Still, she didn't want to completely ruin him, she just wanted to keep him busy for a while, until all the furor died down. "That's a possibility," she said.

"We could catch him in a compromising situation," Allison Petrie suggested.

"I hear he has quite a reputation with the ladies," Margaret said. "If we catch him with the wrong kind of woman that might cause him to lie low for a while."

Lily found that idea downright distasteful. Plus, she

couldn't ignore the current of jealousy that shot through her at the thought of Brian with another woman—especially some sexy harlot with big breasts and the appetites of a nymphomaniac. "We can consider that."

"You know, he has a record," Derrick said.

"He was a singer?" Lily asked. "Now that might be something. I mean, if he imagined himself some kind of rock star and he was really awful, we could get his record played on the local radio stations. That would be really embarrassing."

"Not that kind of record," Derrick said. "A criminal record."

Lily gasped. "Brian Quinn has a criminal record? How do you know that?"

"Mr. Patterson had him investigated after he reported on building code violations on the Minuteman Mall project."

"I read the report," Lily said. "I didn't notice any mention of a criminal record."

Margaret held out a file folder. "This is the latest report from the investigator. It came in this morning and Quinn's got a whole history with the police. They way it looks, the only reason he isn't in jail right now is that his brother is a cop."

"Did you know that Quinn actually had the nerve to crash the benefit that Richard Patterson sponsored last weekend?" Allison asked. "A whole bunch of people saw him there."

Lily snatched the folder up. "From now on, I'd like to be the first person to see the reports from the investigator. Margaret, you make sure that happens. We'll meet again tomorrow morning. I want to brainstorm a few more options."

She opened the folder and quickly scanned the report. There was a complete background piece on Brian's childhood. "We—we can use this," she murmured. Lily glanced up at the four expectant faces staring at her. They were looking to her to take the lead, but she wasn't sure what she wanted to do. Not yet. "We'll meet again tomorrow morning. I need time to look this over."

When Lily got back to her office, she didn't go inside. She wandered over to her assistant's desk and picked up her messages, then flipped through them. There were two from Brian, one with a number she recognized as the station's and the other listed as his cell phone.

"I think he might be calling for a quote," Marie said.

Lily crumpled them up and tossed them both in a nearby trash can. She meant what she'd said! They were virtual enemies on opposite sides of an issue. And she would not put herself in a position to be seduced by the enemy again.

Lily slipped the investigator's report inside her bag. "I'm going to get some lunch," she said to her assistant. "And then maybe I'll walk over to the park. If Brian Quinn calls again tell him that I have nothing to say to him." She paused. "No, just tell him that I'd appreciate it if he'd stop calling. No, wait, don't say that." She shook her head. "Don't say anything. Just take a message."

As she walked out to the elevator, she couldn't contain her curiosity. The report, like the first one she'd examined, was neatly typed and meticulously researched. But this report focused more on Brian's personal life than his professional one.

The elevator opened and Lily stepped inside, joining a crowd of workers on the way down for their lunch hour. When she finally reached the lobby, she hurried outside, into a rush of pedestrians marching down the sidewalk. An unbidden surge of loneliness washed over her, as stifling as the warm, humid air.

Every day she spent in Boston, Lily was reminded that she was a stranger in this town. She had no friends, no one she could confide in, no one who might sympathize with her problems. The only person she felt close to was Brian Quinn and now she'd resolved to put him out of her life for good.

Lily sighed and walked toward the park at Post Office Square, a pretty little oasis in the midst of skyscrapers. When she reached the park, she headed right for the glass fountain and found a grassy spot nearby where she could listen to the soothing sound of water.

She spread the folder on her lap and picked up the report, skimming through it to find mention of the fund-raiser. "According to several guests," she read out loud, "Brian Quinn attended the fund-raiser sponsored by Richard Patterson, held at the Copley Plaza Hotel on Saturday, June 14. He entered without a ticket and was seen dancing with a red-haired woman in a gold dress, her identity unknown to other guests."

Lily took a deep breath, then let it out slowly. There was no mention of what Brian had done after he danced with her, nothing about them leaving together or having sex in the back of her limo. Relieved, Lily flipped back to the first part of the report and began to read. The detective had done a thorough job of describing a rather difficult childhood.

Lily read about Brian's fisherman father and his missing mother, about the difficulties in their home on Kilgore Street in South Boston, the older brother who took care of five younger siblings before becoming a cop. Another brother had become a fireman. "Conor and Dylan," she murmured. "Brendan the writer. Sean is a...private investigator." She frowned. And the youngest brother, Liam, was a freelance photographer. There was also a sister, but Lily skimmed over details of a complex history.

So far, she hadn't found anything that could be used against him. It wasn't a crime to have a bad childhood, an absent father and a mother who deserted the family when he was only three. But then she moved onto the next paragraph and she stopped. "Brian Quinn has several juvenile offences on his record including miscellaneous charges of shoplifting, vandalism, and petty theft. There is proof of an auto theft at age fifteen, but his older brother, Conor, then a rookie cop, convinced the owner to drop the charges." Grand theft auto. Now there was something that his bosses at the station probably didn't know about.

Was she willing to drag his past out into the light? Lily had been forced to play dirty on occasion, but she'd never deliberately hurt another person. And giving the public this information might seriously affect Brian's career. "Knowing his luck, it would raise his popularity," Lily muttered.

Lily lay back on the grass and covered her face with the report, blocking out the sun. She needed to relax and put all her cares and worries aside for a few minutes. Her thoughts drifted, the sound of the fountain in the background soothing her mind. But the images that filled her head weren't of pretty waterfalls and swaying trees. Instead, she saw naked bodies and disheveled clothes, historic scenery passing outside tinted windows. This time, she didn't brush the images aside, but let them linger.

"Imagine my luck."

The voice came out of nowhere and at first, Lily thought it was part of her daydream. But then she realized that she'd dozed off, right in the middle of the park. She slowly lowered the report to find a tall figure standing over her. Though the sun was behind him and she couldn't see his face, she knew who it was. She pushed up, setting the report behind her. "I don't think this has anything to do with luck. I think I must be cursed."

"You, too?" Brian asked. "I guess we have one thing in common."

She glanced up at him and watched his gaze slowly drift from her face to her feet. She wore a business suit, hardly a sexy outfit. But then Lily noticed that her silk blouse gaped open in the front and her skirt was bunched up on her thighs. She quickly rearranged her clothes only to catch him grinning at her.

"May I sit down?" he asked.

Lily braced her hands behind her, trying to ignore the pounding of her heart. Why did he have to be so charming? Even dressed as she was, he made her feel like the sexiest woman on the planet. "No. But you can continue standing there. I forgot my sunscreen and you're providing shade."

"When I was a kid, I dreamed about a career as a

tree," he said, sitting down beside her. He set a paper bag on her lap.

"What's this?" Lily asked.

"Lunch. I called your office and your assistant told me that you were probably in the park."

Lily gasped. "She told you where to find me?"

He nodded. "Right after I told her I was an old friend from college, here in Boston on business. I also told her what a lovely voice she had and that Marie was my favorite name. Hey, I have picked up a few valuable skills as an investigative reporter."

"I still can't believe she did that." Lily tossed the bag back in his direction and got up, tucking the report under her arm before he had a chance to see it. "I have to go." She hurried toward the sidewalk, then glanced back at, to find him smiling at her.

But the smile quickly turned into a frown. He scrambled to his feet and came after her. "Lily, look out for that—"

Her foot caught on something and she looked down and found it tangled in the wheels of a bicycle lying on the grass. She felt herself falling. There was nothing to stop her from tumbling on top of the bike...until she felt a strong hand on her elbow. When she looked back, she found Brian standing next to her.

"Be careful," he murmured. "Watch where you're going." He smiled as he smoothed his palm along her back and she felt her defenses waver. "Come on. Have lunch with me." He walked over and retrieved the bag.

"You're not going to take no for an answer, are you."

"I'm a nice guy. Women have a hard time resisting me." He sat down at her feet and then patted the grass next to him. "I wasn't sure what you liked for lunch," he said as he opened the bag. "After you ordered a salad the other night, I figured you were probably one of those women who eats like a gerbil."

"A gerbil?" Lily laughed as she sat down, thinking about the numerous desserts she had devoured in his name.

"Yeah, one of those little ratlike animals they have in all the kindergarten—"

"I know what a gerbil is," Lily said. She leaned over and looked in the bag. "So did you get me a salad?"

Brian pulled out a sandwich wrapped in paper. "Nope, I got you a grinder." He pulled out a dark brown bottle. "And a root beer." Lily slowly unwrapped the sandwich. "It's really good," he explained. "It has all kinds of meat in it and cheese. Boston is famous for them. In fact, we've taken sandwich-making to new heights."

"Gee, the Pilgrims, the Revolutionary War and now sandwiches," Lily teased. "All we have in Chicago is wind and deep-dish pizza."

Brian shrugged as he twisted off the cap of the root beer. "I thought since you were here, you might want to know something about the city."

She realized her comment sounded awfully cynical. "And what other culinary treats should I sample?" she asked, taking a sip of the soda then smiling as it foamed up in her mouth. He handed her a napkin and she dabbed at her lips.

"Well, you'll definitely want to try Boston Baked Beans. I like to eat those with fish. And New England Boiled Dinner, which is a traditional Irish dish. Since I'm one hundred percent Irish, I grew up on that."

"Really?"

Brian paused. "No, not really. We didn't eat too well when I was a kid. The closest we came to boiled dinner was wiener water soup."

She'd read his file and knew that his childhood hadn't been easy. But it was different hearing the story directly from him. She sensed what it cost him to open up. Brian Quinn, with all his charm and good looks, did not like to appear vulnerable, especially to her. "What is that?"

He grinned. "My family didn't have much money and so we had to make the food budget stretch. If we had the money for hot dogs, then we'd boil them up for dinner and save the water. The next night, my brother Conor would take the water and throw in carrots and potatoes and celery and catsup to make a soup. He wasn't much of a cook, but we learned to like wiener water soup. With Wonder Bread."

"You said your brother Conor did the cooking."

"My da was working and my ma wasn't around. She left when I was three years old." Brian hesitated, as if he wasn't sure whether to go on. "My family came over to the U.S. from Ireland when I was just a baby. I was born there, but I don't remember any of it. What about your folks?"

He'd turned the conversation deftly away from himself, but Lily didn't mind. She could at least give him something in return for his honesty. "They live in Wisconsin," she said. "I grew up in a small town there."

Brian blinked in surprise. "You're a small town girl? How did you end up in Chicago?"

"While I went to college at Northwestern, I interned for DeLay Scoville. They liked me and hired me after I graduated and I've worked there ever since."

"And Boston? How did you end up here...with me?" Brian asked.

Lily met his inquisitive gaze straight-on. "A real estate developer in Chicago hired us to handle his public relations. I was the account manager. He had a little bit of a scandal and I helped minimize the media coverage of it."

"So, you could say you came to Boston just for me?" Brian murmured, reaching out to touch her face. He rubbed her lower lip with his thumb, then stuck his thumb in his mouth. "Mustard."

Lily felt a warm flush creep up her cheeks. "You never give up, do you," she murmured.

"In my business, persistence is a virtue." His gaze locked with hers for a moment and Lily was certain he was about to kiss her. She'd already decided that she wouldn't resist. It was no use. But then Brian glanced down and pulled another sandwich out of the bag and unwrapped it. "You know, if you want a real New England meal, I should take you to a clambake."

"No dates," Lily warned.

Brian sighed. "This is getting old fast. Why not? I don't have anything to hide from you. And I don't care what you hide from me. We're a perfect match."

"No, we aren't."

"We felt pretty perfect that night in the limo," Brian said.

"You shouldn't base anything on that night," Lily said. "That was just...lust. Sex. Nothing more." Though she'd said it before, this time it sounded so cold and calculating. Even if it was just lust, it was incredible, toe-curling, mind-numbing lust. The kind of lust a woman dreamed about.

"You were just using me, right? Any old guy would have done the job. Hell, if I hadn't come along, you'd have invited that...what was he, an insurance sales-man? You would have invited him for a ride."

"No!" Lily cried. "There was a little more to it than that."

"Then it wasn't just about sex?"

Lily squirmed a little under the intensity of his questioning. "There was some attraction," she admitted. "Mild attraction. And I do find you very interesting. Intelligent and witty. And you're handsome, but I get the feeling you know that already." She took a dainty bite of her sandwich. "I'd assumed that the feeling was mutual or you wouldn't have come with me, too."

Brian stretched his legs out in front of him and considered her question. Then he sent her a devilish grin. "Nah, it was just about sex for me."

Lily snatched up the bag and hit him across the chest with it. "You are such a—a jerk."

He held up his hand. "Truthfully? The first time I saw you in that dress I thought, this is a girl I have to meet. You were beautiful, more beautiful than anyone at the party. And when that other guy sat down, I figured you were already taken. But then, you looked over at me and I could tell you needed rescuing. So I stepped in and the rest is history." He paused. "I liked the way your hair fell against your neck, I liked the scent of your perfume and the sound of your voice. And I liked the way you felt in my arms when we danced."

Lily stared at him for a long moment, her sandwich still clutched in her hands. "That's very nice of you to say." She looked away. "But I suspect you say nice things to a lot of women."

"A lot of women don't deserve them like you do," Brian countered.

Lily set her sandwich down and wiped her hand on a napkin. "Have you considered how difficult dating might be? First, we didn't start off the way a normal couple would. And we disagree on some major issues. We'd probably spend most of our time arguing."

"How do we know unless we try?" Brian asked.

Lily sighed. "What if I said I'll think about it and get back to you."

He grinned. "I guess I'll have to be satisfied with that. At least now we're making progress." He rolled over on his stomach and set his sandwich in front of him. "What's this?" he asked.

When Lily glanced over her shoulder, her heart stopped. He had the investigator's report in his hand. He made to hand it to her, then froze, his gaze fixed on the file folder which had his name emblazoned on the front in big block letters. "Give that to me," Lily demanded, reaching out to snatch it from him.

But Brian had quicker reflexes. He scrambled to his feet and walked away from her, reading as he moved. When he finally stopped he was standing next to the fountain. Lily wasn't sure what to do. Maybe it was best he knew how far Richard Patterson was willing to go to protect his interests. If he hadn't found the report first, she might have considered telling him...warning him...as a simple courtesy.

Lily got to her feet and approached him. But before she could explain, he looked up at her with a furious expression. "You had me investigated?" He laughed harshly, then slowly shook his head. "I can't believe this. This is my life. Either you're planning to use this against me or you were a little worried about the man you had sex with." She opened her mouth to explain, but he held out his hand. "Never mind. Whichever it is, I don't want to know."

"I didn't ask for the investigation," Lily said. "Patterson did. He wanted something to use against you."

"This stuff happened when I was a kid." His jaw went tight. "I guess wiener water soup isn't nearly as interesting as my juvie record, is it? Doesn't make for good ammunition. But just think about how the press is going to eat this up—my father was absent and when he wasn't, he was drunk. My mother ran away from home and didn't come back. We lived in a run-down house in Southie that didn't have heat in the winter or electricity when we couldn't pay the bill. Sometimes we stole food from the market just to eat. And all we cared about was staying one step ahead of the social workers. What a pathetic childhood I had. Won't everyone feel sorry for me."

"I'm not going to use this," Lily said.

"No," Brian countered. "Don't back off on my account. Because if you do, I might be tempted to cut you a little slack. We'll just agree that there are no rules. That way, neither one of us can be held responsible for what happens." He glanced around. "I have to go."

Lily watched as he stalked away, the report still clutched in his hand. "I need that report. You can't take it."

Brian stopped short, then slowly turned. His lips were pressed into a tight smile as he approached her. "You need the report." He nodded, then flipped the report over her shoulder. She heard a splash behind her and closed her eyes. "There's your damned report."

She turned to see the report in the center of the fountain, water pouring down over it. And when she turned back, he was nearly to the street. "I thought you didn't care what I hid from you!" she shouted.

Why did every encounter with Brian Quinn seem to end badly? "Maybe it's for the best," she muttered, kicking off her shoes and crawling over the low wall that surrounded the fountain. "If he hates me, then he'll stay away from me. And if he stays away from me, then I won't be tempted to—" She brushed the images out of her head, refusing to give in to another daydream about what they'd shared.

Though the fountain contained no standing water, the shower falling down from the center couldn't be avoided. She held her breath and stepped beneath it, snatching up the report before she nimbly retreated to the other side of the wall.

Water dripped from her hair and the shoulders of her suit were soaked. With a soft curse, Lily smoothed her hair out of her eyes, picked up her shoes and returned to her spot on the grass. Brian had left their sandwiches there, along with the two bottles of root beer. She flopped down on the grass and decided to finish lunch. Maybe by then, she'd be dry enough to return to work.

Lily grabbed up her sandwich and took a big bite. "And he wants to date," she muttered. "I can't spend fifteen minutes with the man before he gets on my last nerve."

5

"I DON'T KNOW what the hell I'm going to do if the report comes out." Brian leaned his head back against the sofa and stared up at the living room ceiling in Sean's apartment.

"Who did the investigation?" Sean asked, flopping down next to him and handing Brian a beer.

"Some guy named Wiffram."

"Harvey Wiffram. He's good. Most of his work is background checks for corporate clients. If there's dirt to be found, he'll find it."

"Everything was in there, Da's drinking, Ma's leaving, the social workers, every petty crime we got caught for. He even interviewed one of my grade school teachers. She made it sound like we were neglected."

"Technically we were," Sean said.

"But we were okay," Brian countered. "I mean, we were taken care of. Conor made sure of that. Things could have been a lot worse."

"So what's gonna happen?"

"They know about the shoplifting. And that little joyride we took with the neighbor's car. That might tarnish the image a bit. I'm worried about Conor. He had to pull some strings to keep us out of jail. And they have all the information about that murder rap that Da had hanging over his head last year. This could put some serious stink on all of us.''

"Why don't you just give up the story?" Sean asked.

Brian frowned. He'd been thinking exactly that since he'd seen the report. But it went against every instinct he had as a journalist. Besides, he was determined to uncover the truth, just to spite Lily Gallagher's efforts.

An unbidden surge of anger raced through him. He shouldn't have been surprised that Lily would stoop so low. Though he hadn't expected her to be as single-minded as he was when it came to her own career, he could certainly understand it. Maybe he'd hoped that their relationship might give her a different perspective on Richard Patterson. It wasn't as if Brian was making the story up. Patterson was a sleazeball.

But to Lily, their attraction was all about animal lust and nothing more. Yes, he'd spent a lot of free time fantasizing about stripping off her clothes and making love to her all night long. There was something about her that could arouse his desire with just the thought of touching her.

It wasn't just lust that drove him, though. He'd always had such control over his desires, able to take a woman or leave her, depending upon his whims. But for some reason, he couldn't let Lily go, couldn't put her out of his head—or his life—for good.

"I'm not going to back off. That's just what Patterson wants. I have to report what I find."

"Is that some kind of rule they teach you in reporter's school?" Sean asked.

"No, it's just part of the job. Conor doesn't walk away from a murder, Dylan doesn't walk away from a fire. And I don't walk away from a story. It's as simple as that."

Sean shrugged and took a long drink of his beer. "Aren't there degrees of importance in your stories?" he said. "Maybe this story isn't as important as you think it is."

Brian considered the suggestion for a long moment. Was Sean right? Had he somehow built this all up in his head? Hell, he'd been trying to break the story for over a year and still didn't have one single shred of solid proof that Richard Patterson had violated any laws. Everyone at the station, including his bosses, would be more than happy if he walked away from it. And if he did, it would solve all his problems with Lily. They could call a truce.

"I can't let it go," he murmured. "Not as long as I think there's something there."

"Maybe she won't use any of that stuff."

"Oh, she'll use it," Brian said. "She's too smart not to. But my guess is that she'll probably save it, maybe wait until I'm just about ready to break the story, then drop it in the media to destroy my credibility. They'll be talking about me instead of the story."

Though Brian wanted to believe that Lily was as coldhearted as that, it was still a stretch. Everything he'd seen in her up to this point had led him to believe she felt at least a small measure of affection for him. Maybe she wouldn't use the report as ammunition. Either way, he'd have to be prepared with a counterattack.

"You need more bargaining power," Sean said as if he'd read his twin's mind.

"And how am I supposed to get that?"

Play the

Lucky Hearts

and get...

2 FREE BOOKS

and a FREE MYSTERY GIFT...

Yes! I have scratched off the silver card.
Please send me my *2 FREE BOOKS* and
FREE mystery GIFT. I understand that I am
under no obligation to purchase any books as
explained on the back of this card.

Scratch Here!

**then look below to see
what your cards get you...
2 Free Books & a Free
Mystery Gift!**

"Find some skeletons in Richard Patterson's closet. Big, nasty skeletons."

"I've been looking," Brian said.

"At his business affairs. You haven't looked into his personal life. Is he cheating on his wife? Does he ignore his children? Does he employ any illegal immigrants? There's a million and one things that might be just as dangerous as what he has on you."

"Can you find something for me?" Brian asked.

Sean scratched his thumbnail over the label on his beer bottle as he considered the request. "Only if you can get me tickets to a Sox-Yankees game next month."

"I can do that," Brian said. "You find me something good to use on Patterson and I'll get you press box passes for the entire series with the Yankees."

The front doorbell rang and Sean jumped up from the sofa. "Pizza's here," he murmured.

Brian grabbed his wallet and tossed it to his brother as he walked to the door. "My treat," he said.

Sean didn't bother to argue so Brian figured he was a little short of cash. He felt guilty asking him to do some legwork for no pay, but Sean didn't seem to mind. He took money when it was offered and worked for nothing when it wasn't.

A few seconds later, Sean returned with the pizza and set it down on the coffee table. Then he went to the kitchen and retrieved two dish towels, throwing one in Brian's direction. "Don't tell Ellie," he muttered. "She'd kill me if she knew I was using her dish towels as napkins."

"Where are Liam and Ellie?"

"They're out looking for an apartment. I told them I'd move out and they could have this place, but with

Ellie's salary at the bank and Liam's new projects, they can afford better. I don't know how I'm going to swing the rent on this place alone."

"You could always move in with me," Brian said. "I've got room."

"Nah. I'd have to leave once you and this Lily woman move in together."

Brian laughed, but it sounded a bit too forced, even to his own ears. "I'm not moving in with Lily Gallagher," he protested. Yet, he wasn't entirely convinced that he hated the idea. He at least wanted a chance with her, an opportunity to see if there was anything behind the passion they shared. Or if that passion would just burn out over time.

"You're not going to have a choice." Sean grabbed a piece of pizza and blew on it to cool it down. "It's the curse. There's no getting out of it."

"But I didn't really rescue her. Her life wasn't in danger. She was perfectly safe." He paused. "Well, there were a few other times that I suppose she might have been in a little danger, and I—in front of the pub the other day, I thought she was about to step out into traffic. And then she nearly tripped down some stairs and there was the bike in the park. I mean, she wasn't really in danger, I was just looking out for her." He paused. "Besides, it gave me a chance to touch her."

Sean took a bite of the pizza. He chewed slowly, pondering Brian's admission. "I suppose you could be right. Conor saved Olivia from Red Keenan's thugs. And Dylan saved Meggie from fire. And Brendan pulled Amy out of the middle of a bar fight. That's pretty big stuff."

"And Liam saved Ellie from a burglar. I saved Lily from a boring evening. It's just not the same."

"But you kind of wish it was, don't you?" Sean asked, raising his eyebrow.

"Right now, Lily and I can't be in the same room without finding something to disagree about. I don't know how the hell that's supposed to lead to eternal love and marriage."

"There must have been something that you liked about her."

"We had very hot sex in the back of a limo. That's a nice little fantasy fulfilled for any guy. And then she told me she never wanted to see me again. Most guys would love that. But I wanted to see her again. I still do."

"Eat some pizza and drink some beer," Sean said. "You'll feel much better. Maybe after we're done we'll head down to the pub and see if we can find you a woman."

Brian nodded. But he didn't want just any woman. The only woman he really wanted was Lily. And though he'd had her once, it just wasn't enough.

LILY SLAMMED THE NEWSPAPER down on the conference room table and glared at the four people gathered around it. "Who leaked this?"

The four suspects—Derrick, Margaret, John and Allison—all looked at her as if she'd just asked who among them had been born on Pluto.

"One of you must have leaked it." Lily picked up the *Boston Herald* and waved it in the air. "Page twelve. There are two columns on Brian Quinn in here. Everything in the P.I.'s report is in the article. It's like they had a copy of it. I thought I told you *I* would decide when to use that information."

"I didn't leak it," Derrick said. He looked at Margaret, his gaze accusatory.

Margaret shook her head. "Me, neither. You took our copy of the report."

"You didn't make any other copies?" Lily asked.

"It just came in day before yesterday," John said. "We barely had time to read it."

"Mr. Patterson had a copy," Allison offered with a weak smile. "He sometimes likes to take things into his own hands."

Lily drew a deep breath and tried to calm herself. She hated to let her temper get the best of her at work. But this was a major mistake. "All right. I'll take care of this. Get back to work. And no contact with the press unless you clear it with me, understand?" She tucked the newspaper under her arm and walked out of the conference room, heading directly for Richard Patterson's office, one story above. When she got to Mrs. Wilburn's desk, she didn't bother stopping. "Is he in?"

"Miss Gallagher, you can't just—"

"Is he in?" Lily asked. "If he is, tell him I need to see him. Immediately."

Mrs. Wilburn snatched up the phone and whispered something into it, then nodded to Lily. "He can see you now."

Lily knew she should have taken some time to cool down, to figure out why she was really angry. Was she upset because her orders had been ignored? Or was it because she knew that the article would hurt Brian Quinn? She'd made it perfectly clear to Richard Patterson that she was the one who would handle media relations. And trashing Brian Quinn in the press was *her* call, not his.

"Lily!" Richard cried as she stepped inside the office. "Did you see the *Herald?*"

"I did," Lily said.

"I would have loved to see it closer to the front page, but page twelve is pretty good. This has got to hurt him."

Lily calmed herself before she spoke. It wouldn't do to shout at him or throw a tantrum. "When I spoke to you last, we made an agreement. I asked you not to interfere, to let me handle things for you and in return I would help you with your little...problem."

Patterson held up in hands in mock innocence. "Hey, I just mentioned what I knew to a friend of mine and he must have gone to the *Herald.*"

"Don't give me excuses," Lily said. "I know what you did. You made a copy of that report and you gave it to a friend who turned it over to someone at the *Herald.*"

Patterson seemed surprised by her insight—and by her apparent lack of respect for his position. But Lily didn't care. Hell, maybe he'd fire her and solve all her problems. Though the job meant big money to DeLay Scoville, if Patterson fired her, she could go back to Chicago without having to admit failure. She could blame everything on a difficult client. "And don't threaten to fire me," Lily added, "because I'll quit before you get a chance."

"Why are you angry? This gives us an advantage."

"If we were going to use this, and I'm not saying we would have, it could have been made public to counteract any report he made. Now, if he airs something damaging to us, I have nothing to use. This is the whole story and in a few days, it's going to be forgotten. They'll have moved on to something new and we'll have nothing."

"I don't think this is nearly as serious as you're making it out to be," Richard said, clearly aware of his mistake now. "So I call the investigator and he digs up more dirt."

"And what if they trace this story back to you?"

"They won't."

"They could. And then, we're going to have to explain why you orchestrated this little personal vendetta against a popular news reporter. It's going to look like retribution and that makes us look petty and vindictive."

Richard sat back down, his jaw tense. "Then do something about it," he muttered angrily. "Just fix it. That's what I hired you for, isn't it?"

Lily nodded, then walked out of the office. She went directly to her own office, grabbed her purse and strode to Marie's desk. "Cancel my appointments for this afternoon," she said. "I'll call in for messages."

"Where are you going?" Marie asked.

"I have to do some damage control."

Lily knew what she had to do and dreaded the prospect. Every time she thought she'd seen the last of Brian Quinn, they got thrown together once again. Maybe, deep inside, she was glad Patterson had leaked the story. Maybe, subconsciously, she wanted to see Brian one last time.

As she rode the elevator down to the lobby, Lily wondered how he had reacted to the article. Had he been angry...or upset? There was no doubt that he was blaming her. She could deal with his anger, but Lily hadn't wanted to hurt him. He was a good man who'd done nothing more than his job. He didn't deserve to have his reputation tainted by his past.

When she got out on the street, she hailed a cab and hopped inside. "WBTN, the television station. It's on Congress. I'm not sure—"

"I know where it is," the driver said. He pulled into traffic and floored the accelerator. Lily held on, trying to focus on what she was going to say once she faced him. Maybe this wasn't such a good idea, she mused. After all, she didn't owe Brian any apologies. Wasn't he the one who said there weren't any rules?

Maybe this *was* all just an excuse to see him again. Lily couldn't deny that she'd been thinking about him. And not just random thoughts. Instead, she'd indulged in very vivid fantasies that involved a general lack of both clothing and inhibitions.

It was almost as if she'd fallen victim to an addiction, unable to deny herself, yet aware that indulging would become more dangerous over time. She needed his touch, needed to taste his mouth and to run her hands over his body. Being with Brian made her feel wicked and sensual and more alive than she'd ever felt with a man before. And though every instinct warned her off, she was like a moth to the flame.

She tried to brush the fantasies from her mind, but they kept returning, making her heart pound a little faster and her blood warm. When the cab finally screeched to a stop in front of the station, Lily was ready to tell the cabbie to turn around and take her back to her office. But instead, she paid him, then slowly strolled to the front doors of the television studio.

The spacious lobby was full of glass and chrome. A receptionist sat at a circular desk in the middle, a bank of television monitors above her head. Lily pasted a smile on her face. "I need to see Brian Quinn. Is he in?"

"Do you have an appointment?"

"No. But if he's in, just tell him that Lily Gallagher is here to see him. He's probably expecting me."

She punched a few buttons on her console, then spoke into her headset. "Lily Gallagher to see you, Brian," she said. She waited for a few seconds. "All right." She glanced up at Lily. "He'll be right out."

A minute later, a door swung open and Brian walked through. Lily felt a tiny thrill rush through her. God, every time she saw him he managed to look even sexier than before. Today, he wore a blue Oxford shirt, unbuttoned at the neck, the sleeves rolled up, and tailored trousers that accented his narrow waist and flat belly.

He slowed as he approached her, then stopped about ten feet away. His hair, usually tidy, looked as if he'd been running his hands through it and Lily felt her own fingers clench as she remembered how the strands felt between her fingers. He watched her warily as she searched for something to say. "Hi," she finally said, certain that was all she could manage for the moment.

His eyebrow arched. "What are you doing here, Lily?"

She glanced around. "Is there somewhere we can talk? Privately?"

"I don't think we have anything to say to each other."

She could tell he was angry. "You saw the article in the *Herald*?"

"So has everyone else at the station."

"Can we please talk? I need to explain."

Brian nodded curtly, then turned and walked through the door. Lily had no choice but to follow. They walked down a long hallway, Lily a few steps behind him. He reached another door and pushed it open, holding it for Lily. She walked into a small room, empty of furniture, the walls padded with carpet. A single window overlooked a control room.

"What is this?"

"It's a sound studio." He reached over and closed the blinds on the window, then turned back to face her. "Say what you came to say," he murmured.

"I'm sorry." Lily clutched her hands in front of her and shifted back and forth. "I know you think it was me, but it wasn't. I had the information, but I don't think I would have used it. I do follow a certain set of principles, no matter what you might believe right now."

"Who leaked the story?" Brian demanded.

"I can't say."

"So your principles don't include telling the truth?" Brian asked.

"Who do you think did it?" Lily said.

"I think one of Patterson's cronies probably leaked the information, carefully, so it couldn't be traced back to him."

"I can neither confirm nor deny," Lily said with a weak smile. "All I can say is that I hope it doesn't cause you too many problems. I've handled situations like these. There may be some talk but it will die down. It's not like you committed murder or had sex with a prostitute. You just possessed a little youthful enthusiasm, that's all."

"They're putting together a damn focus group," he muttered, pacing back and forth across the room. "The station manager pulled me in the minute I got to work this morning. He's worried about my image and the news director is thinking about taking me off the air for a while."

"I'm sorry," Lily murmured, reaching out to touch his arm, her hand trembling slightly.

He stepped back, avoiding her touch. "Do you really care?"

His gaze met hers, and suddenly she knew they weren't just talking about the report. "Of—of course I do. I don't want to see you hurt."

They stared at each other for a long moment and then, as if a bomb had exploded in the studio, they threw themselves into each other's arms. Brian took her face between his hands and brought his mouth down on hers, his kiss hot and demanding. Lily's hands smoothed over his chest, aching to touch his skin.

Nothing seemed to matter but the taste of him, yet even that wasn't enough. He pushed her back against the carpeted wall and pressed his hips into hers, the heat of his arousal evident between him. Lily reached down to touch him there, needing to prove to herself that he still wanted her as much as she wanted him.

Slowly, she stroked him through the fabric of his trousers, his breath coming in hot gasps, his mouth ravaging hers. With a low growl, he brushed her touch away and pinned her wrists above her head, then fumbled with the buttons of her blouse.

Lily moaned as he tore at her bra, pushing it aside to reveal the soft swell of her breast. And then his mouth left hers and drifted down to her nipple. How could she possibly resist these incredible sensations racing through her body? He made her tremble all over, made her ache for his touch. When she was with him, he made her breathless and weak with longing.

But as quickly as it started, it was over. Brian released her hands and straightened, then carefully began to rearrange her clothes. He drew a ragged breath as he turned his attention to the buttons on her blouse. "We can't do this. I'm in enough hot water here."

"Kiss me again," Lily whispered, caressing his cheek.

He did as he was asked, but this time, some of the desperation was gone. This time, he was gentle and sweet. "We can't keep doing this, Lily," he murmured, his forehead pressed to hers. "I want something more."

"What do you want? Tell me and I'll give it to you."

He stared down at her for a long moment. "I want...a date. Something normal. I pick you up, we go out. We get to know each other better, maybe find out if there's something more going on here than just..."

"Lust?" she asked.

"Maybe."

"I thought we agreed that night in the limo that—"

"I didn't agree to anything," Brian interrupted, his jaw tight. He finished buttoning her blouse, then tucked it into the front of her skirt. "You asked me what I wanted and I told you. I'll call you, we'll go out for dinner."

Lily hesitated. This wasn't part of the plan. She knew the dangers she faced in trying to make a relationship work with Brian. When it was just lust, what they shared was simple. But when it was more, then she risked getting hurt. And Brian Quinn was exactly the kind of man who could shatter her heart into a million pieces.

He changed women almost as often as he changed his socks. She'd read it all in the report. He pursued women for as long as they resisted and then cut another notch in his bedpost and moved on. She'd known his type before. But that didn't mean she wasn't tempted.

"All right," she said, reaching for the door.

An instant later, she felt Brian's hands on her waist. He slowly turned her around. His gaze met hers and then he bent close and kissed her again, his hands smoothing over her face as if he couldn't get enough of touching her. And when he was through, he sighed softly. "You go ahead."

"Are you coming?"

Brian chuckled, then glanced down at the front of his trousers. "I think I might need a few minutes—to compose myself."

Lily felt a blush warm her cheeks. "All right. I guess I'll see you then. It's a date."

"I guess you will. I'll call."

BRIAN PULLED UP in front of the Eliot Hotel and scanned the sidewalk for Lily. He saw her standing near the door, chatting with a bellman and he watched silently.

She wore a pretty cotton dress with a loose, flowing skirt that moved in the warm summer breeze. Her hair, a riot of curls, was pulled up into a haphazard ponytail and tied with a colorful scarf.

When the sun hit her, he could see the outline of her legs through the fabric of her dress. "God, she's beautiful," Brian muttered.

He'd been thinking about her all week but had deliberately held off calling her until yesterday. He'd hoped that, given time, he'd be able to understand his attraction to her, and thereby control it. But all he'd learned was that his desire for Lily was completely irrational.

He ought to hate her, or at least mistrust her motives. But the furor over the *Herald* article had died down. He was back on the schedule and according to a station focus group, the article had served to improve his image as a regular guy and a native Bostonian.

So, for now, he and Lily were at a standoff professionally and at a crossroads personally. Maybe after their first date, he'd finally have a clue. Brian beeped his horn and Lily turned to look his way. He stepped out of the car and waved and she came running up. Considering their last encounter in the sound studio, he wasn't sure how it would be between them. But as she came closer, a smile curved her lips.

"Hi," Lily said.

"Hi. Are you ready?"

"I am. But I'm not sure for what."

He circled the car and opened her door for her, grabbing her bag. Before she got inside, he slipped his arm around her waist and pulled her toward him for a quick kiss. She didn't resist, instead tipped her face up and kissed him back. This was how it was supposed to be, he mused. Easy and familiar. By the time he drew away, Brian felt as if they'd smoothed out the difficulties between them, at least for the day. He tossed her bag in the back seat and jogged around to his side of the car.

"Where are we going?" Lily asked, once they'd pulled into traffic.

"It's a surprise," Brian said. "But we're going to have fun, I promise."

"I'm glad you called," Lily murmured. "I wasn't sure you would. I wanted to tell you again how sorry I was for what happened."

Brian shrugged, then reached over and wove his fingers through the tendrils of hair at her nape. "No talk about work today."

"All right," Lily agreed. "So what do you want to talk about?"

"Let's not worry about that," Brian said. "I'm sure we'll think of something."

The drive passed quickly and as Brian suspected, they didn't have any problem finding something to talk about, though he was much more preoccupied with studying her beautiful face than making conversation. Lily chatted about trying to find something to occupy her free time in Boston and Brian suggested things she might try. He didn't suggest his first choice, that she spend every free minute in bed with him. Although he thought it was probably the most valuable use of her time—and her body—Lily probably wouldn't appreciate such brazen talk on their first date. By the time they crossed the Congress Street bridge, he'd nearly convinced her to try sculling lessons on the Charles.

"Sculling lessons," she murmured. "I could do that. I'm really good on the rowing machine at my health club."

Brian pointed out the window at the Children's Museum and the Boston Tea Party ship. "We're heading into Southie now," he murmured. "This is my neighborhood."

"You live here?"

"Not anymore. I have an apartment close to the station. But I grew up here."

"Can we go see the house where you lived? Is it still there?"

"Did I tell you about Southie?" Brian asked.

"I—I just read the report."

"Maybe I should read the report," he teased. "I wouldn't want to repeat something you already know."

"I thought we weren't going to talk about work," Lily said. "Although it will probably be a moot point before too long anyway."

"Why's that?"

Lily shrugged. "I'm thinking of turning this job over to one of the other people at the agency. I'm not sure I can be as effective as I should be."

"You'd leave Boston?" Brian asked.

She nodded. "I shouldn't have come to the station the other day. It shouldn't have bothered me that that story hit the papers." Lily paused. "But it did."

Brian stared out the street, unable to believe what he was hearing. Then with a soft curse, he pulled the car over the curb. "You don't have to leave," he said. "If that's the worst you're going to dish out, I can handle it."

"But I—"

He stopped her words with his lips, yanking her from across the car into a desperate kiss. The thought of her leaving Boston shouldn't have affected him at all. He shouldn't have cared. But he did—and he wasn't sure why. All he knew was that he needed to keep her close for now.

Brian reached up and smoothed his hand over her face. "You don't have to leave. Not on my account. Do what you have to do for Patterson, Lily. I'll understand. No hard feelings."

"You say that now, but it's still going to affect the way I do my job." She laughed softly. "Wait until you meet Emma Carsten. She'll have no mercy. By the time she's done with you, you'll be recommending Richard Patterson for sainthood."

"I thought we weren't going to talk about work," Brian murmured, his gaze fixed on her mouth as he ran his thumb over her lower lip. This was not how he wanted the day to go, caught in a debate about whether she'd be staying in Boston or walking out of his life for good.

"I'll stop talking about work, if you'll tell me where we're going on our...mystery date."

"Well, it involves food and water."

"That's it?" Lily asked.

Brian glanced over his shoulder and then pulled back into traffic. A quick left took them toward the waterfront. He'd been down to the Fish Pier a million times when he was a kid and knew the area well. Though his father offloaded his swordfish catch in Gloucester, the *Mighty Quinn*'s home port had always been South Boston with most of its regular crew coming from Southie.

"Over there is Commonwealth Pier. That's where all the excursion boats leave from." He found a place to park, then pointed straight ahead. "And that's the Fish Pier. Those buildings are almost a hundred years old. This used to be the center for the fishing industry, but not anymore. Commercial fishing has fallen on hard times. There's a plan to develop this area with luxury apartments and a park. Some folks want to leave it the way it is. For the fishermen and all the history."

"Is this the Wellston project?" Lily asked, sending him a suspicious gaze.

Brian shook his head. "No. But it might as well be. It's the same kind of thing. Developers are snatching up waterfront property all over Boston. To them it's just real estate. To the folks who make their living on the water, it's their life. Pretty soon you won't know there were even fishermen in this town." Brian paused. "And now, I'll get off my soapbox. You should be here early in the morning, about six-thirty. They have the fish auction. It's a lot of fun."

"I'd like to see that," Lily said. "Maybe we could go sometime."

They got out of the car and strolled toward the two long buildings that made up Fish Pier. An arcade ran along the street level and Brian remembered playing there as a kid, racing in and out while he and his brothers played tag. He grabbed Lily's hand and drew her toward the building's arch, pointing up at the carving of Neptune's head.

"Some people say that Boston was built by the codfish aristocracy. But there's not much money to be made in commercial fishing anymore. When my da realized that none of his sons were going to follow in his footsteps, I think he was disappointed. That's when he bought the pub." He paused, searching for a change of subject. "That's the No-Name over there. It's a real popular tourist spot now, but when I was a kid, it was just a place where the dockworkers and fishermen ate. They make really good 'chowdah.'"

"Chowder?"

"No, that's not the way to say it," he said with a chuckle. "If you say it that way, they'll know you don't come from *Bahston.* You have to make all your vowels very flat. After we *pahked* our *cah* we stopped at the *bah* for a bowl of *Bahstan chowdah.*"

"Chowder," Lily repeated.

Brian grinned. "Not chowderrrr. Chow-dah."

"Chow-dahr."

Brian pinched her cheeks together. "Chowdah. No 'R'."

"Chowdah," she said.

"Very good." He pointed to a line of boats tied up along the pier. "We're going over there."

"We're going on a boat?" Lily asked.

"Not the *Mighty Quinn.* That's tied up in Gloucester. My brother Brendan just got married and Amy's father bought them a boat for a wedding present. Brendan wanted to take it on a cruise so he asked if we wanted to come along."

When Brendan and Amy had first offered the invitation, Brian had been reluctant to go. But they'd called again and he'd caught himself saying yes, knowing how much he'd enjoy sharing the experience of a warm summer's day on the water with Lily. Though he knew it was a big step introducing her to members of his family, he had his reasons.

Right now, Lily was a fantasy to him, a woman who occupied a secret spot in his life that no one else could touch. They shared an incredible passion. But if he really wanted to understand what was happening between them, then he'd have to look at her in the real world, a world where relationships dissolved and people moved on with life.

As they strolled down the pier, Brian saw Brendan standing on the deck of a shiny new cabin cruiser. He waved, then held Lily's hand as they walked to the boat. "Geez, Bren, this is a step up from the *Mighty Quinn*."

Brian jumped down onto the deck and reached up for Lily, grabbing her waist. He swung her safely down, her body sliding along his until her feet touched the deck. Lily ran her hands over his chest, her fingers warm through his T-shirt. Desire snaked through him, but he quelled it by quickly turning back to his brother.

"I think I'm supposed to call it a yacht," Brendan said. "We asked for a new generator for the *Mighty Quinn* as a wedding present and Amy's father gave us a new boat. I don't think Avery Sloane likes his daughter riding around in an old tub like the *Mighty Quinn*."

Amy, Brendan's wife, stepped out of the cabin. She wore shorts and a tank top and her hair was mussed, as if they'd just gotten out of bed. "Honey, my daddy has ulterior motives. He thinks if he gives you the boat then you'll teach him how to drive it. Then he'll be able to borrow it and take all his business buddies out for an afternoon of motoring and martinis." She glanced at

Lily and held out her hand. "Hi, I'm Amy Aldrich Sl— I mean, I'm Amy Quinn. Brendan's wife."

Brian quickly took up the introductions. "Amy, this is Lily Gallagher. Lily, this is my brother, Brendan. Brendan is a writer and Amy gives away money." He gave his sister-in-law a quick kiss on the cheek. "I could use a few hundred if you've got some laying around."

"Last time I checked, your wallet wasn't a registered charity," Amy teased.

"Brendan and Amy just got married last month," Brian explained.

"Another victim of the Quinn family curse," Amy teased.

Lily frowned. "The Quinn family curse?"

"I don't think Lily wants to hear about our family superstitions," Brian said, slipping his arm around her waist and drawing her closer.

"But I do," Lily countered.

"We'll save that story for later," Brian said. "You can't know all my family secrets. Or was that in the report?"

He watched the smile fade on Lily's face and he instantly regretted what he'd said. The report had become a sore spot between them and Brian should have known to avoid talking about it. Somehow, Amy sensed the shift in mood and grabbed Lily's hand. "Come on, I'll give you the grand tour. Brian said you wanted to experience a real New England clambake."

Lily blinked in surprise. "I—I—"

"Don't worry. The boys are doing all the cooking. We just have to sip drinks and soak up the sun."

Brian watched as they both disappeared into the cabin. Then he turned back to his brother, who watched him with a perceptive grin. "She's pretty," Brendan commented. "Is she the one?"

"The one?"

"Yeah. Did you save her? Family rumor has it that you did."

"Who told you?"

Brendan shrugged. "I think Sean may have mentioned it to Li and Li told Ellie who had lunch with Amy a few days ago. You know how the Quinn family grapevine works. You sneeze in the morning and by dinnertime, we all know you have a cold. I've been thinking about starting a family newsletter so we're all sure we have the facts straight."

"Very funny. Are we ready to go?"

Brendan nodded. "Catch that stern line, then go up to the bow and cast off after I start the engine."

Brian did as Brendan ordered, pushing off from the pier as the engine accelerated. Before long, they were cutting through the water and headed out into the wake left by one of the passenger ferries. It was a perfect Saturday afternoon with just a light breeze and a little chop. He crawled up the steps to where Brendan sat behind the wheel and took the seat next to him.

Brendan handed him a beer. "It's not the *Mighty Quinn*," he said staring at the wide panel of electronic gear.

"No, it's not," Brian agreed. "There's no boat like the *Mighty Quinn*."

"I figure I'll give this back to Amy's father as soon as he knows out how to run it on his own. But for now, I'll have a little fun with it."

"Are you going to live on the *Mighty Quinn* this summer?"

"I don't know," Brendan said. "Doesn't really matter where I live, as long as Amy's there. I know it sounds corny, but—"

"It doesn't," Brian interrupted. He paused. "It doesn't sound corny at all. It sounds nice. Hell, a few weeks ago, I wouldn't have understood what you meant, but I do now."

"You do?"

"Not that I want to spend the rest of my life with Lily. Still, I can see how that might happen...how someone...how *I* might want to settle down. I guess you could say I'm open to the possibility."

"There's just you and Sean left now."

"Sean will never surrender," Brian said. "He's a rock."

"Even Da is softening up. I talked to Keely last week, and she said our parents went out to dinner. Da even sent Ma flowers the morning after. I guess you can teach an old dog new tricks."

Brian's mind flashed back to the conversation he'd had with Sean about their mother's infidelity and wondered if Brendan knew anything about that. "Sean mentioned something the other day that surprised me. He said that Ma cheated on Da. Do you remember that?"

Brendan frowned, clearly surprised by the revelation. "Nah. That can't be."

"I think that's why Sean is so angry with her, why he doesn't want to talk to her. Do you think he saw something?"

"Wow." Brendan slowly shook his head as he stared out at the horizon. "I don't know. I suppose that would explain a lot of things. But I still don't think it's true." He paused. "Sometimes, I wonder what might have happened if they'd just had it a little easier, if he'd just loved her a little more. Da didn't make her life easy. I think about my marriage to Amy and I'd never even consider doing half the things Da did to Ma."

Brian had to admit that he'd harbored the same thoughts himself. He'd always known that love wasn't supposed to be easy. Yet with his brothers, it seemed to be so natural, as if they didn't even have to think about it, never had to doubt their feelings or sacrifice who they were. But with Lily, everything was complicated and unsettled, a disaster waiting to happen. It couldn't possibly be love, so what the hell was it?

They'd shared the most incredible intimacy the night they'd met, stripping away everything but their need for each other. And though he'd known the curves and angles of her body from the start, he didn't really know her. He needed to find out more about the woman who'd made him feel such overwhelming desire. Just who was Lily Gallagher and why did he want her so much?

Today, he'd have his chance to learn. They'd spend the day and evening well chaperoned. With Brendan and Amy around, they couldn't possibly lapse into a passionate interlude they'd regret later. By the end of the day, she wouldn't be some powerful fantasy, she'd just be an ordinary woman, a woman who couldn't possibly hurt him.

Brian stared out at the tiny islands that dotted Boston's harbor. Then, maybe when she left Boston and went back home to Chicago, he could say goodbye without any doubts or regrets. He could put her in the past as he had every other woman in his life and begin again. After all, Lily couldn't be "the one." Could she?

6

THE FIRE BLAZED in the stone pit, sending sparks up into the night sky. Lily snuggled against Brian, wrapped in a rough wool blanket. His arm draped around her shoulders as they rested their backs against a long log on the beach. She couldn't remember the last time she'd been so completely content. She felt...happy. It was such a simple word but it was the only one she could find to describe her condition.

Here, on this little island out in the middle of Boston Harbor, they seemed a million miles away from all the troubles between them. She could almost imagine living like this every day. She and Brian could get to know each other better, they could do things that normal couples did, like eat take-out Chinese and watch videos and argue about the position of the toilet seat.

"I could stay here forever," Lily murmured.

"We could send Brendan and Amy back," Brian suggested. "I'll build you a little grass shack and I'll fish for food—although it's not recommended that we eat the fish from the harbor."

"It's a fantasy," Lily said. "We don't need to think about that. I'll collect sea grass and I'll make plates and curtains and clothes for us."

"Oh, hell, I thought we'd do this thing naked," Brian teased. "Isn't that all part of the fantasy?"

"And what are you two going to do when winter

rolls in?" Brendan asked from his spot on the other side of the fire. "When everything is covered with snow and the temperature is barely above zero."

Amy slapped him playfully. "Don't spoil their fantasy," she said.

"I'm just being practical. Remember our trip to Turkey? We had tents with cots and down-filled sleeping bags and you still had to send me out to buy you more socks from the local market. They're going to dress in grass clothes and live in a hut. Let's get real here."

"You're right," Brian said. "We'll spend summers here, except for black fly season, no-see-um season and the mosquito season. And when it turns cold, we'll go to Tahiti, to our winter hut."

"This fantasy isn't such a fantasy anymore," Lily complained. "If I have to give up Twinkies and Fresca for bananas and papayas, I'm not sure I'll live."

A long silence descended around them, the snaps and pops from the fire the only sounds in the night. Lily sighed, then snuggled closer to Brian. "Hey, why don't you tell me about the Quinn family curse? It's dark, we're sitting around a campfire. A spooky story might be fun."

Brian groaned. "Oh, no, we're not going to go there."

"Why not?" Amy asked. "Lily deserves to know what she's getting into. I'll get the marshmallows."

"I vote we tell her," Brendan said. "She might want to get out now."

Amy pushed to her feet. "First she should hear a *Mighty Quinn* tale, just to put everything in context."

Brian groaned again. "I might as well find the nearest cliff and just jump off. Don't you think the *Mighty*

Quinn thing is more of a fourth or fifth date revelation?"

"A *Mighty Quinn* story," Brendan said in a deep voice. He cleared his throat. "I'll give a *Reader's Digest* condensed version. We begin with a Quinn ancestor, usually clever or handsome or strong, but clearly not living up to his potential. He performs an act of courage or mercy or cunning and suddenly he's a hometown hero. Usually, if there's a woman involved, she's evil, manipulative or greedy. Example, Paddy Quinn plants the magic bean and climbs up the vine to slay the giant, but there's a woman on the ground chopping the vine out from under him."

Lily frowned. "So the stories don't have a happy ending?"

"Oh, always," Brian said. "The *Mighty Quinn* prevails, the dragon is vanquished and the woman turns into a toad. My da thought these tales would teach us to beware of women. They only confused us."

A long silence grew around the fire. "And that's the curse?" Lily asked.

"The curse is a more of a modern-day phenomenon," Brendan explained. "It actually started with our oldest brother, Conor, and then moved to Dylan, then me and then Liam."

Amy returned to the fire and handed Lily the bag of marshmallows. "They played the *Mighty Quinn* and rescued a woman in trouble," she explained. "And they ended up—horror of horrors—in love." She giggled. "Such a sad, sad tale. All those stalwart ancestors protecting the family image only to have this generation turn weak and pathetic."

Brendan growled playfully, grabbed her around the

waist and wrestled her to the ground. Amy scrambled to her feet, then ran toward the water with Brendan following her. "We'll go find some sticks for the marshmallows," he called, before they disappeared into the darkness. Brendan laughed and Amy teased him, her voice echoing in the cool night air. But then their voices faded, replaced by the sound of the water lapping on the shore.

"I think they're still on their honeymoon," Brian said.

"They're good together," Lily said. "That's always the way I thought marriage should be." She hesitated. "Not that I'm thinking about marriage. I mean, I think some people aren't meant to be married."

"Maybe so," Brian said. "I used to think that. But when I see my brothers with the women they love, I wonder if I'm missing something."

An uneasy silence grew between them and Lily wasn't sure what to say. All this talk of love wasn't what she expected from a guy like Brian. "The food was wonderful," Lily said, changing the subject. "Now, I can go home having experienced a true New England clambake. I'll have to send you some deep-dish pizza in return."

"Technically, this wasn't a clambake," Brian said. "More like a lobster boil with a few clams tossed in."

"It was still good," she murmured.

He tightened his embrace and pulled her nearer, nuzzling his face into her hair. "When do you think you'll be going back to Chicago?"

Lily shrugged. "I suppose you'd probably know that better than me."

"Maybe there's a way to keep you here," Brian countered.

Lily looked up at him and he took the opportunity to kiss her, covering her mouth with his and lingering there for a long time. Lily knew she ought to stop, but they'd already crossed the line long ago. Why deny her desire for him? It felt so good to have him close, to feel his hands on her body.

His fingers moved up to her face and traced her features as their kiss spun out, growing more demanding, more passionate with each heartbeat. Lily already knew his taste, the sweet narcotic that was his mouth. A hundred men could kiss her in a dark room, and she could pick out Brian immediately. With him, each kiss was...perfect.

There had been other men in her life, other failed relationships, but when she was with Brian, all those experiences seemed to fade. He'd become something more, a man she *wanted* to trust. Yet there were still so many things standing between them. Though they'd managed a lovely evening together, tomorrow their careers would be back on a collision course.

Brian pulled her down on top of him and Lily drew the blanket over their heads, wrapping them in a warm cocoon of privacy. He stared up at her, his face barely visible in the firelight that filtered through the blanket. "I'm glad I brought you here," he murmured, his hands skimming over her body.

"And I'm glad I came," she said.

"Not bad for a first date."

Lily giggled. "I've had worse."

BOSTON WAS ABLAZE with light as Brian wove through Saturday night traffic in Back Bay. Lily had curled up against his body, still wrapped in the blanket and quietly dozing. He pulled her closer as he waited at a stoplight, then pressed a soft kiss into her rumpled hair. She smelled of salt air and campfire smoke, a scent more intoxicating than any French perfume.

Brian sighed softly, wondering at the oddly protective feelings he had toward her. Though he'd accepted they were on opposite sides professionally, that didn't affect his feelings for her at all. He'd told the truth when he'd urged her to do what she had to do.

But that certainly didn't mean that he was falling in love with her. No, he was a long way from that particular emotion. Lily was simply the most captivating woman he'd ever met. But like the other women in his life, there would come a time when he'd feel compelled to move on—he just couldn't imagine that time right now.

He pulled away from the traffic light and turned onto Commonwealth Avenue, a few blocks from her hotel. How had this happened? He'd dated other women before, even had a few decent relationships. But nothing had ever felt quite like this. No matter how much time he spent with Lily, whether it was an hour or an entire day, it still didn't seem to be enough. Hell, even if they spent a week locked in a hotel room, Brian suspected he'd still want her more than his next breath.

When he pulled up in front of the hotel, he shut off the ignition, then leaned over and gently touched Lily's face. "Hey, wake up," he whispered.

She opened her eyes, then straightened, staring at him as if she wasn't sure where she was. Then she smiled sleepily. "Are we home?"

"We're at your hotel." He opened his door and handed the keys to the parking valet, then walked around to help Lily out of the car. She slipped her arm around his waist and they walked into the quiet lobby. The staff behind the desk and the maid sweeping the carpet nearby barely paid them notice as they walked to the elevators. Brian was going to leave her there, but then decided to walk her upstairs, hoping for a long kiss good-night.

They stepped into the elevator and Lily leaned back against the wall and watched him. He shifted uneasily, wondering if she was thinking the same thing he was—how easy it would be to walk into her room, drag her to the bed and make love to her all night long.

The elevator doors opened on the third floor and they both stepped out. When they reached her room, Lily handed him her key card.

"I should really go," Brian said.

"You should really stay," Lily countered. She took the key back and opened the door, then grabbed the front of his T-shirt and pulled him inside her room. "Just for a little while."

Though he knew he was playing with fire, Brian didn't care. The heat felt good and he wasn't close enough yet to get burned. He growled softly as he dragged her into his arms and kissed her. The door swung shut behind them and they were completely alone, with nothing standing between them and the bed but space. But this time, he wasn't going to let his desire run rampant. This time, he'd enjoy Lily at his own pace.

She began to tug at his T-shirt then moved up to brush his jacket off his shoulders, but Brian caught her hands and drew them up to his lips, kissing the tips of her fingers. "This is our first date," he teased. "I wouldn't want you to think I'm easy."

A tiny smile curled her lips. "I'd never think you're easy." She let her fingers drift down his chest to his belly. "You're very..." She let them drift lower. "...very..." They came to rest below the waistband of his jeans. "...hard."

Brian chuckled. "You look a little tired. Maybe I should put you to bed?"

"I am a little tired," she agreed.

With that, he reached down and scooped her into his arms. A tiny scream slipped from her lips and she giggled as he carried her through the French doors and into the bedroom. He gently set her down on the bed and she kicked off her sandals. "What do you usually wear to bed?" he asked.

Lily frowned. "Pajamas. They're in the bathroom."

Brian walked into the spacious bathroom and found the pajamas, white silk, hanging from the back of the door. He paused a moment to study the things she had spread on the counter, then picked up a bottle of her perfume and sniffed it. It smelled like sunshine, with a slight hint of citrus. As he left, he glanced over at the huge bathtub and wondered if he ought to suggest a bath—just to help her sleep. But that would have to wait for another night.

When he came out of the bathroom, Lily was sitting on the end of the bed. He tossed her pajamas beside her, then pulled her up to stand in front of him. The buttons down the front of her dress were tiny, but he began to work them open.

"What are you doing?" she murmured, leaning into him and running her fingers through his hair.

"I'm getting you ready for bed," Brian said.

"But I don't want to go to bed. I'm not sleepy."

"You fell asleep in the car on the way back here," he said, focusing on the buttons that fell between her breasts.

"That's not the way this dress comes off," she said. Lily reached down and grabbed the hem and in one smooth motion, drew the dress up and over her head. She stood in front of him in her underwear and for a long moment, Brian forgot to breathe. There was no doubt in his mind that she wanted him as much as he wanted her.

He reached out and smoothed his hand along her shoulder, taking the time to memorize the way her skin felt beneath his fingers, enjoying the warmth of her flesh. "You're beautiful," he said.

She watched him as he explored her body with his fingers, testing every soft curve and lean limb until he was satisfied that he knew it all by heart. Brian slipped his arm around her waist and kissed her neck. Lily tipped her head to the side and sighed softly as he moved along her shoulder.

Since that first night in the limo, he'd dreamed about this, about making love to her, taking his time, enjoying the process. But now that he had the opportunity, Brian wasn't sure he wanted to go through with it. Seducing Lily would create more tangles in their already complicated relationship. Having sex just to satisfy a need was all right for a one-night stand. But this had turned into something more, something he couldn't quite define.

Brian's fingers drifted down to the clasp of her bra. He opened it and the lacy fabric fell away, revealing the soft swell of her breasts. A tightly-held breath slipped from his lips as he cupped the warm flesh in his hand. He teased at her nipple with his thumb, bringing it to a hard peak.

Lily tipped her head back and smiled, a silent invitation to take more. Brian sat down on the edge of the bed and spanned her waist with his hands. He hooked his fingers beneath her panties and slowly pulled them down, waiting while she stepped out of them.

His lips found a soft spot on her belly. He'd always had an ideal in his head, the perfect female body, a standard set by numerous men's magazines. But that image had shifted to a woman with soft, feminine curves, with tiny imperfections that made her more real. Lily was that woman with her pale ivory skin, soft as silk, almost luminous in a low light of the bedroom, with her slender waist and curvy hips and perfect breasts.

He wanted to have her then, but something held him back. What was it? Fear? Doubt? Insecurity? When he touched Lily, he felt so strong and aware, as if he could rule the world. But he also felt completely vulnerable, as if she could shred his heart with just one look. If he made love to her now, there would be no going back. He'd fall in love with her as sure as the sun would rise in the east.

"What are you thinking?" Lily asked.

Her words startled him and he glanced up at her, suddenly aware that she was completely naked and he was still dressed. "I was thinking about how soft your skin is." He leaned forward and drew a deep breath, his nose right above her belly button. "And how you always smell like flowers." He paused. "And I was thinking about how I wanted to make you feel."

"Make me feel," Lily said.

Brian smiled, then ran his hands along her hips and over her belly. When he moved lower, Lily sucked in a sharp breath, her eyes fluttering closed. He wrapped his arm around her thighs and pulled her toward him, until she stood between his legs.

As he touched her, she shuddered and he sensed the power he held over her. Brian wondered if she understood the power she had over him, if she knew how hard it was for him to deny his desire. His fingers were damp and slid over her sex, slowly at first, teasing at her desire.

Brian looked up at her, at the smile that curved her lips, the expression, the anticipation that made her even more beautiful than she already was. Her pale skin was flushed a rosy pink and her breasts rose and fell as her breathing quickened.

She held on to him, her fingers clutching his shoulders, her back arched. Her breath caught once, and then again, and she murmured his name. But he didn't want to let her go yet. Instead, he gentled his touch, slowed it, knowing that when she finally came, the orgasm would be more explosive.

Her expression turned intense, focused on his touch. Brian knew she was close and he slipped a finger inside of her, into her damp heat. Suddenly, a shudder rocked her body. A ragged moan tore from her throat and she cried out his name, arching toward his touch.

And then, when it was over, Lily collapsed forward, tumbling them both onto the bed. Her body stretched over his and he felt her breathing gradually come back to normal. Lily laughed sleepily, then pushed up, bracing her hands on either side of his head. "I thought you were putting me to bed."

"I just decided you might need to relax a little bit." He grabbed her waist and then rolled her over beneath him, their legs still hanging off the edge of the bed. Brian kissed her, his tongue teasing hers. "I should go," he said.

"Why? Stay."

Brian sighed. "Why?"

She frowned. "I don't know. Because I want you to."

"That's the only reason I could come up with, too. And for now, I don't think that's enough, Lily." Brian pushed up from the bed and grabbed her pajamas. "Come on," he said, dragging her up to her feet. "I'll tuck you in."

Lily stared at him with an astonished expression. "You don't want to spend the night with me?"

"Oh, I want to," Brian said. "You don't know how much I want to."

"Then why are you leaving?"

"I have absolutely no idea," he said. He fumbled with the buttons down the front of her pajamas, then stepped around her and held the top out. Lily grudgingly slipped her arms through the sleeves. Then he grabbed the bottoms and held them out in front of her. "Just trust me. It's better that I leave. It's our first date. We should at least try to follow some of the rules."

"I don't want the bottoms," she said.

Brian folded them neatly before pulling the bedcovers back. "Hop in," he said.

"Did I do something wrong?"

He chuckled softly. "Everything doesn't always have to happen at warp speed, Lily. You need to slow down. Some things are worth waiting for."

"I usually think that's true. But have you forgotten what we did in the limo that night?"

Brian rubbed her arms. "No. That's not something a guy forgets. But we were strangers then, and now we're not. And this was our first date. I don't think we should sleep together on our first date."

"Considering what you just did to me, I think that's a little ridiculous, don't you?" Lily crawled into bed and pulled the covers up to her chin. "Kiss me goodnight," she demanded. "And promise you'll call me tomorrow morning."

Brian bent over her bed and brushed his lips over hers. "Sleep tight. And I'll take you to breakfast tomorrow. Then maybe we should go to church. I haven't been to confession for a while. I have plenty of sins to tell. Good sins, not bad."

She reached up and touched his cheek with her fingers. "You're a nice man, Brian Quinn. But you confuse me sometimes."

He kissed her once more, then reached over and turned off the light. As Brian stood in the doorway, he looked at Lily, the light from the living room just enough to see that she was smiling. "I don't know what it is about you, but there's something," he murmured.

As he walked to the door, Brian shook his head. This was definitely a first. It wasn't in his nature to walk away from a beautiful, naked woman, especially one who was willing and able to drive him wild in bed. But he had to trust his instincts on this one and his instincts told him that it wouldn't be wise to fall in love with Lily Gallagher. And making love to her tonight would be just that—making love.

For now, he'd need to be more careful.

THE FOURTH OF JULY weekend was especially festive in Boston, a city steeped in the American Revolution. Lily had looked forward to the three-day holiday all week, assured by the hotel staff that it was the best celebration in the entire country. She didn't doubt their enthusiasm as flags flew from every house and lined the major city streets. The city was draped in red, white and blue.

Brian had picked her up at noon, and they'd spent the day walking around Back Bay, window-shopping and sightseeing, taking in some of the spots she hadn't yet visited. They'd had lunch outdoors at a restaurant on Commonwealth, then spent time at a comic book store that also sold silly novelties. Brian bought her a hat with a burst of stars coming out of the top and she wore it for the rest of the day.

The crowds grew bigger as the afternoon wore on, but Brian assured her that they would have a perfect spot to watch the fireworks. Lily couldn't believe it though. The Esplanade along the Charles River was packed with people, their blankets spread out to save a tiny bit of real estate for themselves and their families.

Finally, when it was nearly dark, Brian drew her along through the crowd. They were walking away from the river, but Lily decided to trust him since he was the one who knew Boston best. They got to Beacon Street and he pointed to a four-story house that looked like it had stood on that street for a few hundred years, its brick facade softly weathered by time. "That's it," he said.

"What?" Lily asked.

"That's where we're going." Brian grabbed her hand and drew her along. He opened the front door with a key, but when she got inside, she was surprised to find the elegant mansion completely empty. The interior was stuffy and hot, but as he flipped on the lights, she could see what a beautiful place it was. Nearly every room boasted high ceilings and marble fireplaces, beautifully carved moldings and tall, narrow windows.

"Whose house is this?" she asked.

"My brother-in-law Rafe bought it a couple months ago," he said.

"Why is it empty?"

"He and Keely are going to start to renovate it this summer. They're living in an apartment now."

"Should we be here if they aren't?"

Brian shrugged. "For tonight, the house is ours."

"But it's hot in here," Lily said as she walked along behind him. And though the atmosphere might be romantic, it would be more so with air-conditioning and a little furniture. "Maybe we could open a window?"

"We're not staying inside," Brian said.

They climbed the stairs to the second and then the third floor. And when they finally reached the fourth story, Lily's face was flushed and her spirits a bit wilted. This wasn't exactly what she had in mind for her holiday celebration. But then Brian led her up a narrow stairway and through a door and the entire world opened up. They were on the roof, high enough to see the Charles River and all the people milling about on the Esplanade.

Lily smiled. "This is beautiful," she said. "We'll be able to see everything."

"Yeah, it is," Brian agreed. "Rafe said it would be nice, but I didn't think it would be this nice."

Lily turned to him and threw her arms around his neck. "Thank you." She caught sight of a small table set along the edge of the rooftop deck and she walked over to it. An ice bucket held a bottle of champagne in a puddle of quickly melting ice. Two boxes of old-fashioned sparklers sat next to the champagne. A cooler sat beside the table and Lily bent down and opened it, only to find it filled with food, all of it very elegantly prepared and presented. She pulled out a plate of cheeses and a box of crackers. "Did you do this?"

Brian winced. "If I say no, will you be disappointed? Rafe said he'd put something out for us, but I figured he was talking about a six-pack of beer and a bag of peanuts."

"This was awfully nice of him," Lily said, running her finger along the rim of a crystal champagne flute.

"Rafe is a nice guy. Sometimes I think he feels as if he has to try harder."

"Why is that?" Lily asked.

"He didn't have a very good beginning with the Quinns. And some of my brothers still aren't very comfortable with him. But he married Keely, so he's family now. And he treats her really well, and takes care of my ma, too."

"You'll have to thank him," Lily said softly.

Brian stepped up behind her and wrapped his arms around her waist. "I'll be sure to do just that."

"I'm glad I'm here," Lily said. "I don't know that there's any other place I'd rather be right now."

An instant later, a streak shot into the sky and the first firework of the evening burst in the darkness. Lily's breath caught in her throat as the sky gradually came alive with light and color. They watched for a long time, the sounds of music and cheers drifting up from the river, Brian holding her in his arms as they sipped champagne.

Though she and Brian had seen each other every evening that week, they hadn't allowed themselves any more than a few very long and lingering good-night kisses since the night of their picnic with Brendan and Amy. In truth, Lily had welcomed the new, less complicated direction of their relationship, their silent plan to start back at the beginning. It hadn't changed her desire for him. She still ached for his touch and craved his kisses. But their new relationship was like dieting—though it meant a constant state of starvation, it was good for them both.

But here, with the fireworks bursting over their heads and the champagne making her nose tickle, she didn't feel quite so confident. It would be so easy to give in to desire. When Brian touched her, she lost all ability to resist. A tiny shiver skittered through her as her mind flashed back to that night in her hotel room. The things he'd done to her, the control he'd had over her body, still made her blush.

Lily knew that if she turned around and kissed him right now, she could convince him to make love to her, here on this rooftop. But things had changed between them, a subtle shift in her feelings. When she'd first met Brian, she'd been simply overcome by lust. But now, there was something more to their relationship.

She groaned inwardly. Relationship. That's exactly what she'd vowed to avoid. But there was no denying it any longer. She and Brian had crossed over from one-night stand to a...relationship. She should have felt guilty about giving up so easily on her plans for a romance-free life in Boston, but when he kissed her, she'd been forced to admit that she was probably lost before she'd ever really gotten started.

Still, Lily couldn't ignore the fact that sooner or later, they'd have to face what was happening to them and make some decisions. She sighed inwardly. Just the thought of that discussion filled her heart with dread. She had her life in Chicago, he had his in Boston.

When the fireworks were over, they sat on the roof and finished the champagne, talking softly as the crowd below them headed for home. But the day had been long and the wine only served to make Lily sleepy. She yawned and stretched her arms above her head, willing to sleep right where they were, beneath the moonlit night sky.

"Come on," he murmured. "I'll walk you back to the hotel."

Lily smiled. "I'm not letting you put me to bed unless you're willing to crawl in with me."

"Tempting," he said. "But then you wouldn't get any sleep."

"That's the point," Lily said. She stared at him for a long moment. "What are we doing?"

Brian reached out and slipped his hand over her

nape, toying with her hair. "I don't know, Lily. But whatever it is, we're having fun, aren't we?"

"Yeah, we are," she agreed. "But I'm just not...I don't know..." She shook her head, unable to put her confusion into words.

"It's all right," Brian murmured, brushing his mouth against hers. "We don't have to figure it out tonight, do we?"

They walked back through the house, turning lights off as they passed. When they reached the street, they headed toward Commonwealth Avenue, walking slowly, their arms around each other. People still crowded the streets, heading toward the T stations and the bus stops, their arms filled with blankets and lawn chairs and picnic coolers.

Lily wasn't sure she'd ever spend another Independence Day without thinking about her night on a Boston rooftop with Brian Quinn. She glanced over at him, still amazed by how sweet and handsome and funny he was. Giving in to an urge, she pulled him into the doorway of a shop and wrapped her arms around his neck, kissing him long and hard.

Brian chuckled, then dragged her back out on the sidewalk, pressing a kiss to her forehead. "We're never going to get you home if you keep doing that." A woman stumbled into them and Lily held out her hand to keep her from falling.

"Miss Gallagher?"

Lily gasped as she recognized Richard Patterson's secretary, Mrs. Wilburn. Of all the people to run into tonight! The only person who might be higher on her list than Richard Patterson's loyal and devoted secretary was Richard Patterson himself.

Mrs. Wilburn glanced over at Brian, her gaze coming to rest on their hands, still clasped together. Lily swallowed hard and gently tugged her fingers from his. "Mrs. Wilburn, this is—"

"I know who you are," Mrs. Wilburn said, her expression unreadable, her eyebrow raised slightly.

"Brian Quinn," Lily finished.

"Did you enjoy the fireworks, Mr. Quinn?" Mrs. Wilburn asked.

"I did," he said. "We did. We watched from a rooftop on Beacon Street. They were really good this year. More...colorful, I think."

"Yes, well..." She turned back to Lily. "I'll see you at the office on Monday, Miss Gallagher. Have a pleasant weekend."

When she was out of earshot, Lily groaned then leaned back against a nearby fence post. "Oh, God, she knew we were together. She's going to tell Patterson. She's going to tell him and then he's going to fire me. I'm consorting with the enemy—in the truest sense of the word."

Lily started off down the street, weaving through the crowd. Brian quickly caught up to her. "I'm sorry, Lily. I suppose I could have just walked off, but I think she saw us together and it might have looked like we were trying to hide something."

"No!" Lily said. She stopped and turned on him. "I've spent the last week pretending that this wasn't standing between us. I actually thought I could separate my professional life from my personal life and I was doing a pretty good job of it. But we were both just kidding ourselves. We knew this would blow up in our faces at some point, so why not admit that we've reached that point."

"Lily, that's not what—"

"Why haven't you pushed your story about Patterson?" she demanded. "You've backed off, haven't you? Is it because of me?"

"No," Brian said. "I've just been working on other stories."

She drew a shaky breath. "Well, here's a news flash. Next week, we're doing the ground-breaking for the Wellston waterfront project. We pushed it up a month thinking that if we just did it, then the media would finally realize they can't stop us. As a media professional, I'd advise you to get your story on the air before people forget about the waterfront and the fishermen and start thinking about how nice it would be to eat at one of those fancy restaurants we have planned."

"Why are you telling me this?" he asked.

"Are you going to run your story?"

"Yes. When I'm ready."

"Then we'll be ready for you when you do."

"Since when is it 'we'?"

"I work for Richard Patterson," Lily said. "I represent his interests, first and foremost. That's my job, remember? And if Mrs. Wilburn tells him about what she saw, he's going to consider it a betrayal and I'm going to lose my job. A job I need to pay for the damn house I just bought." She paused, calming her anger. But her frustration couldn't be contained. "You don't care about my life, do you? All you care about is what we shared that night in the limo."

"What? You think I deliberately walked in this direction knowing that we'd run into Patterson's secretary on the street? It's a bad break, but we'll deal with it."

"You'd get everything you wanted in one easy step. I'd get fired and there will be no one to refute your story."

"You're being irrational, Lily. I don't want you to lose your job. And I don't care if you counter the story with one of your own. It's just a job. It's what we do to pay the rent. It doesn't have anything to do with what we feel."

Yes, she was being irrational. But it had everything to do with what she felt. Lily couldn't ignore the fact that losing her job would suddenly destroy the barriers that stood between them. There were times when she'd been ready to quit, to put her little battle with Brian Quinn behind them and explore the feelings they shared. But she needed her job. It was who she was.

This was all happening too fast! She was ready to give up everything she had worked for to have a man she barely knew. A man she wasn't sure she could trust. "I—I have to go. I'll talk to you later."

"I'll walk you back," Brian said.

Lily shook her head. "No, I need some time to think. Time to figure out how to handle this."

"Fine," he murmured.

To Lily's relief, he didn't fight her. She started down Commonwealth Avenue, moving along with the pace of the crowd, but not really watching where she was going. She wanted to feel angry, to lash out at Brian for everything he'd done to mess up her perfectly ordered life. It was his fault she'd lost control. If he hadn't been so sweet and sexy and—Lily cursed. It was *his* fault!

Lily stopped on the street and covered her face with

her hands. All right, she was partially to blame. In truth, maybe this whole thing was her fault. She'd invited him into the limo that wonderful, incredible night—a groan slipped from her lips. Her life was falling apart and all she could think about was spending the rest of her life in bed with Brian Quinn!

"Get a grip," she muttered. "He's still the enemy. And I'll be damned if I'm the one who's going to surrender."

7

THE DAY WAS ONLY HALF-OVER and Lily was completely exhausted. She sat in her office, her shoes off, her feet tucked beneath her, staring out the window at a gloomy sky. Lightning flashed in the west, signaling the approach of a summer storm. If she were home right now, she'd have called in sick, curled up in bed, and had a nice little pity party for herself.

Her mind wandered back to Friday night and then to the last week she'd spent with Brian Quinn. When she'd first learned who he really was, Lily had known any contact with him would be dangerous. But she couldn't seem to resist him, no matter how hard she tried. He was sweet and sexy and charming and he made her feel like she was the only woman in the world.

But things were different between them now. Since running into Mrs. Wilburn, Lily couldn't think about Brian as the man she desired. He was the enemy again—an enemy responsible for ruining her professional reputation. Whatever happened, Lily was ready for it.

At least the confusion would finally come to an end. She'd know exactly where she stood. Lily had even pushed the issue with Brian, telling him about the ground-breaking, taunting him into running his story. From a business standpoint, it hadn't been the best move, especially if she managed to keep her job. But she was sick and tired of having his story hanging over her head. Sometimes it was better to face a problem head-on than try to figure out how to handle it if and when it came.

"It is all for the best," she murmured, rubbing her temples with her fingers. "Whatever happens." With a soft curse, Lily reached for her phone and punched in a familiar number.

"DeLay Scoville Public Relations," the receptionist said.

"Emma Carsten," Lily said, deepening her voice so that the woman wouldn't recognize her. She waited for her friend to answer. "Hi, Em. What's going on in Chicago?"

"Lily! I've been hoping you'd call. I went over to your house and watered your plants and picked up your mail. Everything is fine, but someone stole the pot of geraniums you had on the front stoop. What do you want me to do with the mail? There's a ton of junk and lots of magazines. And a card from your mother."

"I don't know," Lily said. "Hold on to it for now."

"All right." A long silence spanned the distance between them. "What's wrong, Lily? You sound a little bit upset."

Lily bit her bottom lip. Normally, she wouldn't hesitate to confide in Emma. But now that she found herself in a tangle of personal and professional troubles, maybe Emma wasn't the best person to tell. After all, she was a loyal employee of DeLay Scoville and wasn't the most objective observer. "I don't know. I'm starting to think I shouldn't have taken this job."

"Are you crazy? How could you refuse? DeLay almost wet his pants when he saw that retainer check. He's been talking about you ever since you left, how great you are, what a bright future you have at the agency. He's about to crown you 'Consultant of the Year' and put your name on a damn plaque in the lobby."

"But I'm not sure I can handle this, Em."

"Is it that bad? What did Patterson do? Is he in big trouble? He didn't give anyone a cement overcoat, did her?"

"No!" Lily cried. "He's not a mobster, at least I don't think he is. It's not even Patterson. It's..." Lily gnawed on her bottom lip. "You know, if I had a family emergency, maybe I could convince DeLay to send you out here. You'd love Boston."

"Lily, what's going on? You can tell me."

Now that she was ready to confide, Lily wasn't sure how to explain what had been happening to her. When she'd come to Boston, she'd been determined to change her life, to quit dreaming of romance and avoid unavailable men. The problem was, she'd had a one-night stand with a man who was perfectly available. That had been her big mistake.

Still, there were a whole host of problems beyond that. They were too much alike, too driven, too single-minded when it came to their careers. Though their passions made for an incredible fire between them, it also spelled disaster for a lasting relationship. And there was always his rather long and colorful history with women.

"I'm just...I don't know. Maybe I'm homesick."

"For Chicago? Then why don't you come home? You

can spend next weekend here and fly back on Sunday evening. I could use your help."

"With work?" Lily asked.

"No, I'm sanding the floors of my apartment and it's turning into a nightmare. I've been walking around for the last week covered in a thin coating of dust."

"I think I'll do that," Lily said. "I need to be in familiar surroundings for just a little while. " She hesitated, knowing that the conversation was winding down. "I—I met this man, Em. His name is Brian Quinn. He's a reporter. An investigative reporter for a television station."

"And?"

"And nothing. I'm just a little confused."

"Wait," Emma said. "Oh, Lily, don't tell me this. He's working on a story about Patterson, right?" Her friend groaned. "I don't know how you manage to pick the worst guy in the world to fall in love with."

Lily squirmed in her chair. Trying to explain her attraction to Brian Quinn over the phone was impossible. Emma needed to see him to know what Lily was up against. "I didn't know who he was when I met him. I should have broken it off as soon as I found out. I knew it was doomed, but I couldn't seem to let it go. He just...does something for me. And I was curious to know how long it would last." She swallowed hard. "And now, I think I may have to give up this job. I have a serious conflict of interest here."

"What is this 'it' you're talking about? Are you having a relationship? Are you having sex?"

"Kind of," Lily said.

"The way I see it, you have two choices," Emma said. "One, you can dump the guy and focus on your work and come back here and have the job of your dreams. Or two, you can call DeLay, tell him you want out, he'll fire you and you'll lose your house and your car and never be able to buy another pair of designer shoes in your entire life. What's it going to be?"

Now that Emma laid the options out so clearly, Lily could see the choice should be quite easy. "There is one other option. Richard Patterson finds out I'm dating Brian Quinn and *he* fires me and then Don DeLay fires me. And then my life falls apart."

"Do you honestly think that's a possibility?"

"If I get fired, we could always start a firm of our own, like we've talked about. Wouldn't that be a great idea? Carsten Gallagher Public Relations. I'll even give you top billing."

"Lily, don't bother coming home this weekend. I'm going to come visit you. We'll shop, we'll have lunch and we'll get this straightened out."

A knock sounded on Lily's office door and she turned away from the window. "I have to go," she said. "I'll call you tonight and we'll talk more. Bye, Em." She hung up the phone and drew a deep breath, fully expecting to see Richard Patterson on the other side. "Come in."

Marie opened the door and stepped inside. "There's a delivery for you, Miss Gallagher. Do you want it in here?"

"Of course. Is it that media report I sent for?" Lily asked, rearranging the folders on her desk.

But when Marie reappeared in the door, she held a huge bouquet of flowers, a beautiful mix of pink and cream-colored roses. "It's really pretty. There's a card. Would you like me to read it?"

"No, I know who they're from."

Lily stood, took the flowers from Marie and set the vase in the middle of her desk. "They are pretty." She took the card and slid it out of the envelope. Scrawled in a masculine hand was a message from Brian. *Missing you,* he wrote. *Dinner tonight?* She forced a smile, then slowly sat down, her view of the door completely obscured by the size of the bouquet.

They hadn't spoken since the night of the fireworks and Lily had almost hoped he'd stay away. She'd spent the entire weekend trying to focus on anything that would take her mind off Brian Quinn and her impending termination. And she'd nearly convinced herself that whatever happened, she'd deal with it—alone.

If she only knew how she really felt about Brian, then she might have considered a future with him. But her history with men made it hard for her to trust her own feelings, much less the feelings of a man she barely knew. Yes, there was an undeniable attraction between them, but it wasn't love!

"Mr. Patterson's secretary just called," Marie said. "He wants to see you as soon as possible."

A knot tightened in Lily's stomach and she suddenly felt nauseous. "Fine, Marie. Tell her that I'm on my way."

Mrs. Wilburn was a loyal employee. It wasn't a surprise that she couldn't keep something like this to herself. Patterson would fire her and then DeLay would fire her and her life, as she knew it, would be over. Lily's heart slammed in her chest. She'd never been fired before. She wasn't sure what to expect.

Lily hurried to the elevator, but then noticed the Out Of Order sign. As she trudged up the steps, she wondered if she should make a preemptive strike. If she quit before Richard Patterson had a chance to fire her, then at least she could say she'd resigned. She wouldn't have a black mark on her resume.

She approached Patterson's office and Mrs. Wilburn gave her a haughty look, then nodded. "He's ready for you," she murmured. "You can go in."

Lily knocked softly on the door then stepped inside, preparing herself for the worst. But when she saw Richard sitting behind his desk, he was grinning. Lily returned his smile hesitantly. "Good morning."

"Sit," Richard said. "I just wanted to catch up with you and tell you what an outstanding job you're doing."

Lily stifled a gasp. "Thank you," she murmured, trying to hide her complete astonishment.

"Mrs. Wilburn told me that she saw you with Brian Quinn, Friday night. She was quite bothered, but I've always said 'Keep your friends close, and your enemies closer.' I'm glad to see that you're willing to do what's necessary to keep an eye on him."

"Of—of course," Lily replied.

He cleared his throat. "Now, I don't care to know the details, but the fact that you're willing to go...the extra mile is admirable. Keep him distracted. Good plan." He smoothed his hands over the surface of his desk. "So, carry on. Do what you have to do."

"Right," Lily said. She turned and walked out of the office on wobbly legs, then continued past Mrs. Wilburn to the stairwell. When she reached the stairs, she willed herself to calm down. "This is just perfect," she muttered. "I didn't lose my job and he doesn't think I'm a traitor. Instead, he thinks I'm a slut."

Lily groaned and sat down on the first step. Well, she now had official permission to have another night or two of hot sex with Brian Quinn. Lily pushed to her feet. So why did that suddenly seem like the last thing she wanted to do?

BRIAN WALKED INTO the diner and glanced around at the patrons seated for an early lunch. The place was a favorite hangout for media junkies, offering quick lunches and bottomless cups of coffee and 24-hour CNN on the television. There were plenty of empty spots at the counter so he grabbed a stool and sat down, figuring he and Sean could snare a table when his brother arrived.

He ordered a Coke, then pulled out his cell phone from his pocket and punched in Lily's number at work. But, before the phone rang on the other end, he hung up. He needed to let Lily deal with her business problems on her own. Since he'd left her Friday night, he'd been preoccupied with worries about her. She had been so upset when she'd walked away, so certain that being seen in public signaled the end of her career.

Brian grabbed a menu and stared at it. He didn't want to see Lily hurt, but there was no denying that his interest in her was causing a problem—in both their lives. Last week, they'd spent nearly every free moment together. It hadn't taken long for Brian to realize that his feelings for Lily ran deep—much deeper than simple lust.

He'd never meant to fall in love, but he was coming dangerously close to doing just that. He looked forward to seeing her and felt restless when she wasn't near. He loved the sound of her voice and the way her face lit up when she smiled. And when she touched him, every nerve in his body came alive.

Brian closed his eyes and drew in a deep breath, then tried to focus on the menu again. He'd call her after work and hopefully, her worries about Mrs. Wilburn would have been eased or maybe forgotten entirely. "Or maybe, she'll be out of a job and looking for someone to blame," he murmured to himself.

"You're Brian Quinn."

The man who spoke sat down next to Brian and Brian sighed inwardly. He'd just wanted to have a quiet lunch. But with his face on the side of every bus in Boston, it was tough to walk around unrecognized. He reached into his pocket for a pen. Hopefully all the man wanted was an autograph. He turned and smiled. "Yes, I am."

The man sat down on the stool beside him. "I saw your report on that building inspector who was taking bribes. That was great work." The man held out his hand. "I'm Jim Trent. I'm the city editor over at the *Globe*."

Brian tried to contain his surprise. "Hey. It's good to meet you. I read the *Globe*. I love the *Globe*. I used to work at the *Globe*."

"You did?"

"Yep, when I was in high school and college. I used to load the trucks. But that was more than ten years ago. You weren't there then. Marcus Reynolds was city editor. He was great, but I think you're doing a better job. Harder hitting pieces, tighter writing."

"Maybe. But let me tell you, I don't like what I see coming from you. You've scooped us on almost every story you've done this last year. We should have had those stories."

"That's my job," Brian said.

"You're good on camera, but how are you on paper?"

"What are you asking?"

"Are you a writer or just a face?"

"I worked at a couple newspapers, in Hartford, Connecticut, and Burlington, Vermont, before I took the job at WBTN. I thought I was a pretty good reporter. I still write every word of my copy. Why? Are you offering me a job?"

"I've got a spot for a staff writer who can make things happen," Trent said. "Are you interested? You'd have to start at the bottom."

Brian didn't want to appear too interested, but inside he could barely contain his enthusiasm. The *Globe* was one of the best newspapers in the country, right up there with the *New York Times* and the *Washington Post*. He'd be starting at the bottom all over again, but he'd have a chance to prove himself by his work and not his pretty face.

"I am," Brian said. "But this has to stay between us for now."

"When does your contract with the station expire?"

"Six months," Brian said. "But they're already starting to renegotiate. My agent isn't going to like this. A job at a newspaper won't pay his commission."

Jim held out his hand and Brian shook it. "I'll be in touch," he said. "Or you call me." He clapped Brian on the shoulder. "Before I leave, you wouldn't want to tell me what you're working on now, would you?"

"If I tell you all my secrets, you won't want to hire me."

"Hey, I know all your secrets. I read the *Herald*." He turned and walked out the door, pushing it open just as Sean walked in from the street. Sean saw Brian immediately and strode over. "Buy me lunch," he said, slapping a large manila envelope on the bar.

"Why should I buy you lunch?"

He pointed to the envelope. "Check it out."

"What is this?"

"You wanted something to use against Patterson, to pay him back for that article in the *Herald*. There it is. Nice and juicy."

Brian opened the envelope and withdrew a stack of eight-by-ten glossy photos. At first, he wasn't sure what he was looking at—until he recognized Richard Patterson's face...and his chest...and his naked ass! Brian shoved the photos back in the envelope. "Where the hell did you get these?"

Sean rolled his eyes and grabbed the envelope. "You didn't get to the good ones." He pulled out the stack and flipped through the photos until he came to one in particular. He showed Brian a photo of a naked Patterson with an equally naked woman.

"So he and his wife like to walk around the house in the buff," Brian said. "That's not news and I'd be laughed out of town if I reported it."

"That's not his wife," Sean said. "And that's a sleazy little no-tell motel out on Route 28. You can tell by the television. You have to feed it quarters to get porn. Poor man's pay-per-view."

"Who is the woman?"

"I don't know," Sean said. "I was hoping you could

tell me. I followed her home the other afternoon. They meet every other evening from about five until seven. He leaves from the back entrance of his office building and takes a company car. She drives a black Mercedes and lives at the same residence as Dick Creighton."

"Creighton?" Brian let out a tightly-held breath. "Louise Creighton is head of the planning commission. She ultimately decides what gets built in Boston and when." He stared at the photo again. "That's her." Brian laughed. "That's Louise Creighton."

"He buys her jewellery," Sean said. "Expensive stuff. He bought her diamond earrings last week."

"Geez, Sean. This is incredible. Do you know what this means? I have the link. I know how Patterson is getting his approvals. Man, this could be the scandal of the year. And I've got photos!"

"Can we order lunch now?" Sean asked. "I'm starved."

Brian reached in his pocket and withdrew his wallet, then motioned to the waitress behind the counter. "Run this through," he said, he said, offering his credit card. "I'm paying for my brother's lunch. Give him anything he wants. In fact, give him five of everything he wants. And add a tip for yourself."

Brian grabbed the envelope, then hurried out to the street and hailed a cab. He gave the driver directions to Patterson's office building. For the second time in ten minutes, Brian punched her number into his cell phone and asked for Lily when the receptionist answered. When he heard her voice, he couldn't help but smile.

"Hi, it's me. How's it going?"

"Surprisingly well," Lily said. "I still have a job."

"I need to see you. Can we have lunch?"

She hesitated. "I can't. Brian, I don't think we should see each other anymore. I have to focus on my job."

"This is important. I need to talk to you now. I promise, this is strictly business."

"All right."

"I'm in a cab about five minutes away. Be out front." He paused, fighting the urge to tell her how he felt. What was he supposed to say? I think I'm falling in love with you? How the hell was he supposed to be sure? "I'll see you in a bit."

Brian flipped off the phone, then tipped his head back and closed his eyes. Maybe he shouldn't worry. The way things were going with the rest of the Quinn boys, he probably didn't have much choice in the matter. If the curse had struck again, he'd realize his true feelings sooner rather than later.

But then, he was only seeing this from one angle. Lily had a life in Chicago and for now, she still had a career. He might fall in love with her, but the curse didn't necessarily force her to feel the same way. "It's too early," Brian murmured. "Or maybe, it's too late."

The cab pulled up to the curb a few minutes later and Brian asked the driver to wait. He stepped out and saw Lily, then waved at her. When she hurried up to him, he pressed his palm into the small of her back. "Come on," he said.

When they were in the cab, Brian leaned forward. "Take us over to Storrow Lagoon on the Esplanade." The cabbie pulled back out into traffic and Brian immediately slipped his arm around Lily's shoulder and pulled her in for a kiss. "I've been thinking about that all morning," he murmured.

She bit her bottom lip. "You promised you wouldn't—"

"So, what happened?" Brian interrupted. "I assume that Mrs. Wilburn kept her mouth shut."

"No. She told Patterson and he called me in. He thought I was using my feminine wiles to...influence your pursuit of the story. You know, trading my body for your silence."

"He said that to you?" Brian asked.

"Not in those words, but it was implied. And encouraged. So I guess we have a green light. We could go get a hotel room right now." She laughed, but it sounded forced. Lily folded her hands on her lap. "So, what did you need to talk to me about?"

"Not right now," Brian said. "I just want to kiss you, then we'll talk." He reached out and ran his thumb over her lower lip, his gaze fixed there. "Do you want to kiss me, Lily?" He touched her lips to his, gently teasing with his tongue.

She opened beneath his gentle assault, but Brian felt as if she were holding something back. He'd kissed Lily enough to be able to read her feelings, to sense her emotions. And Lily didn't taste happy to him. Hesitantly, he drew back, then grabbed her hand and wove his fingers through hers.

The cab dropped them off near the lagoon and they walked across the grass, his hand still clasping Lily's, the other holding the envelope filled with pictures. The lagoon was one of the prettiest places along the Charles River. Across the lagoon, a slender island was connected to the river bank by little stone bridges. On a warm, sunny day, children usually sailed toy boats in the water, but today's windy and threatening weather had driven most people closer to shelter.

"Every day you show me a place that's prettier than the last," she murmured.

Brian pointed to a bench. "Let's sit."

Lily took a spot on the far end, sitting just far enough away so that they wouldn't touch. Brian took a deep breath. He wasn't sure whether he was doing the right thing, but he'd know in a few seconds. Brian handed her the envelope and watched while she opened it. As Lily flipped through the photos, her eyes grew wider and wider.

"Where did you get these?"

"That doesn't really matter."

"Are you going to use them?"

"That's the head of the planning commission with him. It makes the connection I need. It's only a matter of time. He'll be up for bribery of a public official and he'll probably go to jail. I just thought you might want to know."

"Why?"

"I don't know. So you can be prepared," Brian said. "This is going to get messy, Lily. I just want us to come out all right on the other side."

She stared down at the photos. "There's no way I can...I can't tie a ribbon on this and make it look good." She stood. "I have to go."

"Lily, let's talk about this. You have to understand. He's breaking the law. I have to report the story. If it were just unfounded suspicions then I might be able to sweep it under the rug, but in a few days, I'm going to have all the proof I need."

"Do what you want," she said. "I'm finished." She

started back toward the street and Brian jumped up and followed her.

"What do you mean, you're finished?"

"I'm going back to Chicago. I've got the ground-breaking in a few days and then I'm packing my bags and leaving. They can send someone else to clean up the mess."

Brian frowned, grabbing her hand and spinning her around to face him. "You can't leave."

"I can. I'll just quit. It's really quite simple. My boss will assign someone else and they can deal with the problem. And you can report your story and gather your awards."

"No," Brian said, his temper rising. This wasn't like Lily. She didn't give up so easily. But she looked so defeated, as if the photos had taken the last ounce of fight out of her.

"This is for the best," she said. "Really. From the start we knew we were on opposite sides. I just don't see any way that we can both come out of this with our integrity intact. I should have stayed away from you from the start. I should have been stronger."

"Lily, I didn't give you much of a chance."

"This is the way it's always been. I just pick the wrong kind of guy. There's always something. They always look good on the surface, but then sooner or later, I find out the truth. I thought if I tried a different approach, I wouldn't get hurt. I guess it didn't work either." She started off again toward the street, but this time when Brian went after her, she turned and held out her hand. "Just let it go. It's for the best. Really, I'm fine."

Brian watched her walk away. He wanted to follow

her, to find some way to work this all out. But though his heart was willing, he knew in his head that they'd just go round and round and come out in the same place all over again.

"So much for the Quinn family curse," he muttered.

THE OFFICE at Patterson Properties and Investments was quiet, the lights were dimmed and the sounds of the cleaning crew drifted through Lily's open office door. It was nearly seven, but she'd been working on the media kit for the Wellston waterfront project, readying everything for the official ground-breaking on Friday afternoon. She'd made contacts with all the news organizations and made sure that any questions would be answered in the media kit. And now, all she had to do was wait...and hope.

Lily reached into her desk drawer and pulled out a bag of peanut M&Ms. She dumped a pile on her desk and popped a few in her mouth, the chocolate immediately calming her cravings. A few days ago, the only cravings she'd had were for Brian Quinn. And now, she'd gone back to sweets. "I'll weigh two hundred pounds, but at least I won't have a broken heart," she murmured.

Lily had been waiting all week for some story—any story—to hit the news, for Brian Quinn to finally reveal his case against Richard Patterson. It was like waiting for an earthquake. She knew it would come sooner or later, but she wasn't sure just how bad it would be when it did. Lily had prepared contingency plans for every possibility, ready to jump to Patterson's defense at a moment's notice.

It was best that she'd decided to break things off

with Brian. She'd ignore his messages and avoid seeing him and pretty soon, she'd wouldn't think of him at all. Lily shook her head. It was a nice little delusion, but right now, that's all she had to hang on to.

Her phone rang and Lily noticed it was her direct line. She hesitated before picking it up. She hadn't given Brian the number, but she had given it to Emma. Emma, Lily mused. She could use the advice of her best friend. She snatched up the phone. "Lily Gallagher."

"Miss Gallagher, this is the security desk downstairs. I have a gentleman here to see you." The man lowered his voice. "It's Brian Quinn, the news guy."

"Tell him I'm not in," Lily said.

"I'm afraid I can't do that." The guard cleared his throat, then whispered again. "He's standing right here."

"I'll be right down," Lily said. She dropped the phone back in the cradle, then stood and smoothed her skirt. As she walked to the elevator, she thought about what she should say, how she should explain. She'd experienced her share of breakups, but she'd always been on the receiving end. An ultimatum might work—choose her or his story. She knew he'd choose the story and it would be over between them.

"That seems too simple," Lily muttered. "But sometimes, simple is better." She walked to the elevator and punched the button, shocked when the doors actually opened up in front of her. She stepped inside and rode down, all the while telling herself to be strong. But the moment she saw him standing in the lobby, her resolve wavered.

He wore an immaculately pressed shirt and pleated

trousers, his usual work attire minus the coat and tie. In all honesty, Lily thought he looked pretty amazing in just about anything he wore. She frowned. With all the intimacies they had shared, she'd yet to see him completely naked. Her heart skipped at the thought of slowly undressing him. He would be so beautiful to look at—to touch.

They slowly approached each other and Lily found his expression impossible to read. He didn't look angry, but he also didn't look happy to see her. "Hi," she murmured.

Brian grabbed her hand and drew her back toward the elevators, away from the prying ears of the security guard. "What the hell is going on here, Lily?"

"I don't know what you mean."

"I call you at the hotel, you don't answer. I leave messages at your office and you don't reply. What's with you? If you're blowing me off, then at least tell me to my face. Don't make me figure it out on my own."

Lily drew a ragged breath. "We've had a wonderful time together, but—"

"I'm not going to use those photos on the air. Hell, I'm not even going to report that they're having an affair."

"You aren't?" she murmured.

"What do you want from me Lily? Either we're going to do this or we aren't. It's up to you. Personally, I think we're pretty good together. I've never met a woman quite like you."

"You know it will have to end sometime," Lily murmured. "If it's not this story, it will be something else."

"Maybe. But maybe not. We won't know until we try. And I want to try."

She glanced up at him, surprised at the admission. She'd just assumed that he was taking their little affair much more casually than she was. Every instinct warned her to walk away. If he broadcast his story about Patterson, they would be forced to battle each other in the media, no holds barred. And if he didn't, she'd be done with her work and on her way back to Chicago next week.

"What if I asked you to give up the story about Patterson?" she asked. "Would you do it?"

Brian opened his mouth to reply, then snapped it shut. He considered her question for a moment longer. "I thought we agreed we were going to keep our professional and our personal lives separate."

"That's what we said. But I can't put things in little compartments. This is my life and if you're a part of it, then you're part of all of it. And if you're not, then you're not."

"What are you asking, Lily? Whether I will make the choice? Or whether I want to make the choice."

She straightened, then shook her head. His answer was obvious. "I'm asking you to stop calling. To just...stay away. I had a wonderful time with you, but from the start, I wasn't looking for something...serious."

"Ah, hell," Brian said, turning away from her and raking his hand through his hair. "I do not want to have this talk right now. Neither of us should be making any decisions. It's too soon."

"I have to go," Lily said. "I still have a lot of work to do and you've probably got to get to the station tonight." Her hand trembled and she longed to reach out and touch him just one more time, so that she could remember what his skin felt like beneath her fingertips.

"I'm doing the report tonight," he murmured.

"What? But you told me—"

"I edited it this afternoon. We have film of Patterson and the planning commissioner coming out of a motel room. We're going to run it. That's what I came here to tell you. I'm telling you now. Tomorrow, it's going to be all over the news. I hope you're ready."

She straightened her spine and tipped her chin up. "I will be." With that, Lily turned on her heel and strode back to the elevator, then punched the button emphatically. That was it. The end of everything they'd shared. She'd almost been grateful that she hadn't been forced to choose. She bit back a sob, unwilling to give in to her emotion.

The elevator doors opened immediately and she stepped inside, praying that they'd close just as quickly. Brian watched her for a long moment, his gaze fixed on hers, and then at the last instant, he stepped inside as well, the doors closing behind him.

"What are you doing?" Lily asked.

"We're not finished yet."

He punched the button for the 20th floor and the elevator started up. But Lily reached around him and pushed the button for the lobby, intending to ride right back down again. "This doesn't have to be all messy and emotional," she said.

"Maybe it should be," he said. "Maybe you shouldn't be able to just end it without at least some sort of discussion."

A grinding sound filled the elevator and Lily looked up. "What was that?" The sound stopped suddenly and then, so did the elevator. It bounced a few times and Lily waited for the doors to open, but they didn't.

Brian pushed the button for the 20th floor again, but the elevator didn't move. "I think we might be stuck."

"No!" Lily cried, punching every floor between one and twenty. "We can't be."

"I think we are." He opened the door beneath the control panel and pulled out a phone. "Do you want to call or should I?" He pulled the phone away as she reached for it. "Or maybe we shouldn't call. This might be Fate lending a hand. And I'm never one to mess with Fate."

8

LILY SAT in the corner of the elevator, her legs stretched out in front of her and crossed at the ankles. She glanced over at Brian who sat in the opposite corner, his gaze fixed on her legs. He looked up and realized that she'd caught him staring.

"You have nice legs," he said. "It's not against the law to look."

Lily tugged on her skirt, pulling it down to just above her knees. "When are we going to get out of here?" she muttered.

"We've only been stuck for fifteen minutes," Brian said. "It'll be soon." He glanced at his watch. "It better be soon. I have to get to the station."

"Maybe this *is* Fate stepping in—to keep you from broadcasting that report."

"Or maybe it's the lack of decent elevator repairmen in this city," he countered.

She shouldn't even be talking to him, Lily mused. After everything she'd said outside the elevator, it was almost hypocritical to act like nothing had happened once they were trapped inside. She'd called an end to their relationship once and for all, and now, she'd have to do it all again.

"I'm hungry," Lily said. "I didn't have dinner."

Brian reached into his pocket and produced a box of

breath mints. "That's about it. You're going to have to make them last."

"How long do you think we'll be in here?"

"The security guy said it would be at least an hour before they got a repairman over here. So why don't we make the best of our time?" He grinned. "Wanna play five questions again?"

Lily rolled her eyes. "All right. But we each get two passes."

"You first," Brian said.

"Are you really going to air your story tonight or did you just tell me that to see how I'd react?"

"I'm really going to air it—if I get out of here in time. My turn. Are you really going to walk away from us or did you just tell me that to see how I'd react?"

Lily sighed. "I meant what I said." She thought about her next question. "Any regrets?"

He nodded slowly. "I have a few regrets."

"That's not a good enough answer. Tell me what they are."

Brian stared down at his shoes. "I regret that I never got a chance to make love to you the way I really wanted to," he murmured. "What about you? Do you have any regrets?"

Lily hesitated. They were telling the truth here. Why not be honest? "I was thinking that I'd never seen you...naked," Lily said. "We've shared such intimacies but we've never been completely intimate with each other."

"That can be remedied." Brian reached for the buttons of his shirt and Lily realized that maybe honesty hadn't been the best policy.

"Don't you dare."

"Why not? As long as we're stuck here, we might as well be comfortable. And I don't want to leave you with any regrets." He yanked off his shoes and socks, and Lily was certain that he was only teasing, certain that he'd stop there. But he returned to his shirt and unbuttoned it from top to bottom.

It gaped open, revealing a tantalizing view of muscle and skin, a broad chest with a light dusting of hair that ran from his collarbone to his belly. Lily felt her fingers twitch as she remembered touching him down there. Though the sight of him had started her heart racing, she tried to appear calm, as if men undressed in front of her on a regular basis.

Brian stood and began to unbuckle his belt. When he was finished, he pulled it from the loops and dangled it in front of her face.

"Hey, don't entertain me," she said. "Play to the camera."

"The camera?"

Lily pointed above her head to a clear glass window above the control panel. "Security camera," she said. "They can see everything you're doing."

Brian glanced up, then pulled his keychain from his pocket. He used a tiny pocket knife to unscrew the panel, then grabbed his sock and covered the camera lens. "Complete privacy," he said.

The phone rang and Lily giggled. "Complete?"

Brian grabbed the phone and answered it. "Yeah, she's here." He handed to the phone to Lily. "It's the guard."

"Miss Gallagher, are you all right? Something has happened to the security camera."

"I'm fine," Lily said. Her eyes went wide as she

watched Brian shrug out of his shirt and drop it on the floor beside her. "Just get us out of here."

"It's going to be at least a few hours," the guard said. "Are you sure you're all right? If I have to, I can call in the fire department. They could force the door and—"

"No," Lily said, suddenly realizing that maybe she wanted to stay. "That won't be necessary." She handed Brian the phone and he hung it up. "Two hours now."

"There's a lot we can do in two hours," he said. He held out his hand. "Come on."

"I'm not taking off my clothes," Lily said.

"We can dance. There's music." He gently pulled her to her feet. "We were good at dancing, remember?"

Lily did remember—she remembered how it had felt that first time he'd touched her and how dancing had been a prelude to seduction. He pulled her into his arms, and the moment he did, she knew she'd made a mistake. Her breath dissolved and for a moment, she wasn't sure she could draw another. She suddenly felt dizzy and weak.

His chest was so smooth and warm as she slid her hand up to his shoulder. The music piped into the elevator played softly and they moved along with it.

They'd known each other for nearly three weeks now, but there were times when Lily felt as if she'd known him her whole life. She felt comfortable in his arms, as if she somehow belonged there all along. But she'd made so many mistakes with men in the past, been fooled so many times. She let her head rest against his shoulder. If they could just stay here, alone in the elevator, everything might work.

The music never ended so they continued to dance,

his hands lazily drifting over her body, his fingertips discovering something new with each touch. There was no use fighting the desire. They were trapped together for two hours. If she didn't give in to him now, she'd surely capitulate later.

But this time, she was going to let Brian set the pace. She wanted to be seduced and she knew if she let him, he'd give her a night she'd never forget—even if it happened to be in an elevator.

As they danced, he slowly removed her jacket and tossed it on the floor with his discarded shirt. Easy listening wasn't exactly the best accompaniment to their striptease, but then her intimate encounters with Brian Quinn had never been conventional. Piece by piece, they finished undressing each other, after each item aside, taking time to explore what had just been revealed.

When he'd skimmed her panties over her hips and down her legs, Lily felt oddly vulnerable. Before this, it had always been about lust. But this was different, so slow and easy and deliberate. Though she wanted the passion, she also hungered to feel close to him, to somehow touch his soul this time. If this was the last time, then she wanted to experience it fully and without hesitation.

He pulled her against his body and Lily lost herself in a deep, soul-shattering kiss. She could barely breathe and when she tried to think, her mind was occupied with the wild sensations racing through her body. "I can't believe we're doing this," she murmured.

"Dancing naked in an elevator? Been there, done that," Brian teased.

"You have not," she said.

"No, I haven't. I'd never made love in a limo either. Or watched fireworks from a rooftop. Or drank champagne from a woman's navel."

"We never did that," Lily said.

"Then I guess we have something to look forward to."

Lily groaned inwardly. Why did he have to be so damn romantic? Why couldn't he be like every other guy on the planet—aloof, self-absorbed, distracted? She hadn't wanted to meet the perfect man, she'd just wanted a tidy little one-night stand. And here he was, making her feel all these things that she didn't want to feel, making her believe in the possibilities of love.

He caught her chin with his finger and tipped her face up until she met his gaze again. He kissed her, gently at first and then with greater conviction. The kiss spun out, each moment filled with unquenchable desire. It had always been like this between them, first gentleness, then giving way to unbridled passion.

Lily moaned softly as he traced a line of kisses from her neck to her shoulder to her breast. His tongue teased at her nipple, drawing it to a hard nub before he moved to her other breast. She tipped her head back and enjoyed the shivers that raced through her. But Brian didn't stop at her breasts. He dipped lower, to her belly, then lower still, making love to her with his tongue.

A tremor shook her body and for a moment, her knees went soft. She couldn't think, she couldn't speak, she couldn't stand, but yet she was aware of every sensation that pulsed through her. It had always been so easy for him to bring her pleasure. She barely had to take a breath before the knot in her belly tightened and she gave way to her release.

But this time, he didn't bring her all the way. Instead he drew her closer and closer to the edge, then eased her away. Lily's breath came in ragged gasps as she leaned back against the elevator door, the metal surface cool on her back. Her eyes fluttered open and she watched him retrieve a condom from his wallet on the floor.

Even if he hadn't had protection, Lily wasn't sure she could have resisted. Not now. She needed to feel him inside her again, needed the heat and the hardness and the final surrender. Needed to assure herself that what she was feeling was real. He gave her the condom after removing it from the package and let her sheath him. As she smoothed it over his erection, Brian closed his eyes and sighed softly.

When he opened his eyes again, she saw a look there that caused another shiver to race through her. He wanted her and nothing was going to stand in his way. Brian lifted her up and wrapped her legs around his waist, then pressed her back against the wall of the elevator.

He stood for a long moment, his face nestled into the curve of her neck. "You don't have to ask," Lily murmured. "I want this as much as you do."

He probed at her moist entrance then slowly slipped inside of her. The sensation of him filling her with his heat was more than she could take. It hadn't felt this way the first time. There had been pleasure then, but not this intense longing. Lily groaned, shifting herself until he touched her very core.

Brian moved slowly at first but Lily was so close and

with every thrust she risked tumbling over the edge. She murmured his name, but she wasn't sure if he heard her. When he softly bit her neck, she knew the pain was the only thing keeping her in the present and she relished the reminder.

Lily furrowed her fingers through his hair and brought his lips back to hers, whispering soft pleas against his mouth. She kissed him, her tongue matching each thrust, desperate to taste him. And then, like a sudden cloudburst on a sunny day, Lily felt herself tense and convulse around him. A shower of pure pleasure washed over her body and a moment later, he joined her, driving into her hard, moaning her name.

She wasn't sure how he managed to remain standing, but he did, still kissing her softly as her breathing came back to normal. He opened his eyes and stared down at her. "I'm in love with you, Lily."

She reached out and pressed a finger to his lips. "Don't say that."

"I have to. It's the only thing I know for sure right now, except that I don't want this to end. I don't expect you to feel the same way, but I wanted you to know."

An uneasy silence fell over the elevator and she fought the temptation to return the sentiments. It would be so easy to tell him that she loved him, but she'd said those words before and they'd only come back to haunt her—and hurt her. "Everything has to end sometime," Lily murmured.

He slowly lowered her to the floor and they sat on the scattered clothes, Lily curled up against his naked body, a sheen of perspiration causing her skin to chill. He stroked her arm with his hand, a lazy caress that seemed wonderfully possessive. Then he grabbed his shirt and wrapped it around her, drawing her back against his body.

They sat silently, both lost in their own thoughts. Lily wasn't sure what to say to him. Right now, her mind was a mass of confusion and conflicting emotions. Maybe she did love him and she just didn't realize it. Or maybe she wanted to love him but wasn't capable. Or maybe this was still all about sex and nothing more.

How could she be sure that he loved her? Had he really meant what he'd said, or was it just a response to what they'd shared? Questions swirled in her head and she closed her eyes, searching for an answer, any answer.

Suddenly, the elevator moved, jerking once, then restarting. She looked up at the lights above the doors and noticed they were going down. With a soft cry, Lily scrambled to gather up her clothes. Brian helped her slip into her blouse and handed her her skirt, but she stuffed her underwear in her pocket.

And then, to her horror, the elevator stopped and the doors opened on the lobby. They both looked up to find the elevator maintenance man staring at them, his tool belt hanging from his waist and his mouth agape. "They're all right, Barney," he shouted.

Brian, still completely naked, grinned, and shifted slightly to shield Lily's body from the man's view. "We'll be right with you," he murmured, reaching out to hit the "close door" button on the panel.

Lily fumbled with the front of her blouse, rebuttoning it twice before she got it right. "So, I guess you're going to be able to air your story tonight. If you hurry, you'll make it to the station with plenty of time to spare."

"No," he murmured.

"But I thought—"

"I just told you that to see your reaction. It's not ready yet." As he held his finger on the button, he kissed Lily again. "Remember what I said, Lily. And think about it. We could be great together."

A CROWD OF REPORTERS had gathered at the construction site. Brian recognized vans from the other three network stations in Boston and watched through the window as the reporters chatted with each other. As news went, a ground-breaking was a pretty minor event. But this project had had a high profile from the start. Brian couldn't seem to stay away—but it wasn't because of the news value.

It had been three days since he'd last seen Lily, since the evening they'd spent trapped together in the elevator. After everything she'd said to him, and everything they'd done to each other, Brian was even more certain that they belonged together. But convincing Lily of that fact had turned into a near impossibility.

He cursed the men in her life who had made her so distrustful. Though she'd never told him about her past, Brian sensed that she'd been hurt, and not just once or twice. He was loath to believe that he'd be another name on that list. But the choice had been hers, not his. He'd admitted his feelings for her and now it was up to her.

"What time is this supposed to start?" Brian asked.

Taneesha held out the press release. "Three p.m.

sharp. Why are we here? I thought you'd already edited this piece."

"I'm not happy with it yet," Brian said. "There's something missing."

"Hello," Bob said, peering out the front window of the news van. "What's this?"

Brian stood between the two front seats and watched as a line of vehicles drove onto the property. As each one stopped, five or six people hopped out, each of them carrying a sign and a plastic garbage bag. Brian chuckled. "We have a protest. Maybe this is worth covering."

"Who are they?" Taneesha asked. "And what's with the garbage bags?"

"They're commercial fishermen," Brian said. "And dockworkers." He caught sight of a familiar shock of white hair. "Aw, hell, that's my da out there." Brian yanked the side door open and jumped out of the van. "Set up outside. I think this might get interesting."

Brian wove through the growing crowd of people, their signs clearly putting them in opposition to Richard Patterson's plans for the waterfront. He caught up with his father just as Seamus Quinn was shouting directions to a group of dockworkers.

"Da!"

The older man turned, then broke into a grin. "Hey, boyo! Are you here to put us on the news. Make sure you shoot me from my good side." He grabbed a wizened old man and pulled him over. "You should talk to Eddie here. He used to operate a fishing boat right off that pier over there, the Maggie Belle. Brought in the biggest load of codfish in Boston fishing history. When was that, Eddie?"

"That would have been 1952," Eddie said.

"What's in the garbage bags, Da?"

"Never you mind," Seamus said.

Brian shook his head. "Don't do anything stupid, all right? I'm not going to have time to bail you out of jail."

The crowd began to shout and Brian turned and saw two black limousines rumbling down the dusty road. The reporters moved in a swarm to catch Richard Patterson as he emerged from the car. But Brian was waiting for someone else. Lily stepped out of the next limo, frowning as she took in the unruly crowd of protesters and the clamoring reporters.

Apprehension niggled at Brian's brain. He didn't like the way things were beginning to look. The protesters seemed a little too volatile and the reporters were more interested in the protesters. He tried to catch Lily's eye, but she moved closer to Patterson and whispered something in his ear. Then they walked toward the small stage that had been set up at the head of the pier.

"Save our waterfront!" the crowd began to chant. "No more development!"

Lily forced a smile as she stepped in front of the microphone. But just as she began to introduce Richard Patterson, all hell broke loose. Something flew out of the crowd and hit the podium. Brian rushed forward and more objects whizzed through the air in the direction of Patterson. It was then he realized the protesters were throwing dead fish—and from the smell, they were more than a few days dead.

"Go back to the van," he shouted to Bob. "Taneesha, keep the tape rolling."

Brian shoved through the crowd of protesters as they surged toward the podium. The reporters backed away, not willing to risk a close encounter with a rotten fish. Richard Patterson had already disappeared behind a wall of bodyguards, but he'd left Lily to fend for herself, dodging and ducking flying fish.

Brian reached her a few seconds later and she was still trying to calm the crowd. "Come on," he shouted. "You've got to get out of here."

"No!" Lily said.

With a low curse, Brian grabbed her legs and pulled her off her feet. She fell over his shoulder and he carried her through the crowd to the news van. Bob slid the door open as Brian approached.

"Put me down!" Lily shouted, kicking her feet. "I can handle this!"

"The hell you can," Brian said.

"Brian, put her down!" Seamus shouted just outside the van. "Don't you go actin' the hero. You know what happens."

Brian ignored his father and the rotten fish that hit him on the shoulder. Lily screamed as another fish hit her head. When he reached the van, Brian dropped her inside, then climbed in after her.

She brushed the hair out of her eyes and glared at him. "What do you think you're doing?"

"Saving your pretty little butt," Brian said.

"I can't let these people scare me," Lily said. "You have to stand up to protesters. If you wanted to help me, why didn't you call the police so they could arrest them all and throw them in jail."

"Isn't security your responsibility?" Brian asked.

"After all, this was your ground-breaking ceremony, not mine."

"You're enjoying this, aren't you," Lily snapped. "This is just great news for you."

"You think I wanted to come to your rescue?" Brian asked, his anger getting the better of him. He'd just dragged her to safety! The least she could do was thank him. "I might as well have tied an anchor around my neck and thrown myself off the end of the pier. Now I'll have to marry you."

Lily gasped. "What?"

"The curse," Brian said, raking his hand through his hair. "I save your life and that's it. It's all over. The curse. There's no going back now."

"Don't be ridiculous. You didn't save my life. No one ever died from getting hit by rotten fish."

"Well, I saved you from danger. More than once. About five or six times by my count. That all adds up."

"And you think that means I'm going to marry you? You're crazy."

"You won't have a choice in the matter," Brian said. "It's already been decided."

Bob cleared his throat. "Would you like me to leave?" he asked.

Brian ignored him, fixing his attention on Lily. "It's not such a bad idea, you know. You can't deny that there's something between us and it's more than just sexual attraction."

Lily shook her head. "You're wrong. And you know you're wrong. This is all just about the pursuit. You're going after me just like you go after a story, no holds barred. But once you get me, you'll just move on to something new, someone prettier or more interesting, someone who can hold your attention for a little longer than I could."

"Lily, that's not true."

"I am going to leave you two alone," Bob said. He opened the driver's side door to the van.

"No!" Lily cried. "I was just leaving." She jumped out of the side door and started through the crowd of protesters toward the second limo that waited, the fish flying again. Brian watched her, ready to jump to her aid if anyone tried to stop her. But the protesters were happy enough to have broken up the event and limited themselves to a few derisive shouts in her direction. She crawled in the limo and it quickly sped away, the tires kicking up a cloud of dust on the gravel road.

"Did you just ask her to marry you?" Bob inquired.

Startled out of his thoughts, Brian glanced to the front seat of the van. "No."

"Are you sure?"

"I told her I was going to marry her," he murmured. "I didn't ask. There's a difference."

"IT WAS A FULL-ON DISASTER," Lily said. "Rotten fish everywhere. It's been all over the news. And there was a photo of me on page nine of the *Herald*. Actually, not me but my backside. My very big backside."

Lily grasped the newspaper as she paced back and forth in her office. After yesterday's horrific ground-breaking ceremony, she had scrambled to cover all the public relations ramifications. She'd issued a statement to the press touting Richard Patterson's belief in the right to protest, yet his determination to see the Wellston project move forward. She'd answered questions from reporters and analyzed media coverage of the

melee. Everything seemed as if it would be all right—
until the *Boston Herald* hit the newsstand.

"It can't be that bad," Emma said, her sympathy di-
minished only slightly by the distance between them.
"You always have a tendency to exaggerate when
you're upset."

"He threw me over his shoulder and carried me off
the stage," Lily said.

"Who? Patterson?"

"No, Brian Quinn. It was so...mortifying. The *Herald*
got a photo and now, the news media is all over it. Two
stations ran tape of it on their noon news and not in the
news segments either. They're using it as humor.
There's one piece of tape that shows me getting hit in
the head with a rotten fish. Before I know it, that tape
will end up on one of those bloopers shows." Lily
moaned. "And that's not the worst part."

"There's worse?"

"I think he may have asked me to marry him. I'm not
sure. I mean, it wasn't a traditional proposal. He tossed
me into his news van and said we had to get married."

"This guy sounds like he's a few sandwiches short of
a picnic. He hauls you around like some caveman, then
demands that you marry him. Lily, what do you see in
a guy like that?"

"Oh, that's not the way he is," Lily explained. "He's
usually so sweet and considerate. But he's also dangerous." She paused. "And funny...and he's smart, really
smart."

"It sounds like you're in love."

"I'm mostly confused," Lily said. "And maybe a little in love."

"A little?"

"Yeah," she admitted, pleased with the thought. "Or maybe I'm just in love with the idea of being in love. It's been so...intense between us, so passionate. I didn't think I was capable of such desire. But the rational side of me knows that this will all fade over time and I'll discover that I'm not in love. Or maybe, it won't fade and he'll discover he's not in—"

"Stop trying to overthink this. Do you or don't you love him?"

She ignored Emma's question, unable to answer it at the moment. "I've already written my letter of resignation. I can't be effective here. I'm a joke."

"Lily, don't make any rash decisions. Don't react emotionally. Isn't that what you always tell your clients? Take some time, see how things play out. Maybe they aren't as bad as you think."

Lily stared down at the newspaper, at the awful photograph. "Oh, they're bad, all right. If you'd like to come to Boston, I can recommend that you replace me. I think I can talk Patterson into keeping the agency on, but with another account manager. And maybe, if I can do that, I can save my job at DeLay Scoville. If not, Gallagher Public Relations will be launched and I'll be eating a lot of peanut butter sandwiches and buying my designer shoes at K-Mart."

A soft knock sounded on her office door and Marie poked her head inside. "Mr. Patterson would like to see you," she whispered, a worried expression on her face.

"Thanks, Marie." She sent the girl an encouraging smile, then turned her attention back to Emma. "I have to go. I've been summoned. Wish me luck."

"You won't need luck, Lily. Everything will be just fine."

Lily hung up the phone, then slowly stood, taking a last look around her office. She'd already gathered what few personal items she'd brought along and packed them in a bag, just in case. But as she walked to the door, Lily found herself strangely calm.

This all seemed part of some grand cosmic plan. The way Brian talked, they'd been destined to be together from the moment they'd met. Though it was a wonderful fantasy, that was all it was. As soon as they put some distance between them, this overwhelming attraction would fade. It was all about lust and not about love. Lily was honest enough to admit that to herself.

She walked out of the office to find Marie hovering near her desk. "Miss Gallagher, is everything all right?"

"Probably not. But you don't need to worry. It's not your fault."

Lily moved toward the elevator and waited. But the moment she stepped inside, she realized that she should have taken the stairs. Her mind flashed back to the night she and Brian had been caught inside. What had ever possessed her to make love to him in an elevator? She'd lost all sense of professional and personal decorum since she'd arrived in Boston.

But as the doors opened up, Lily couldn't bring herself to step out. She remembered the words he'd said to her and how hard it had been to believe him. Did he really love her or was it just the passion of the moment that had brought the sudden declaration? The doors began to close and she quickly stepped out, putting that night behind her for good.

Mrs. Wilburn was coldly efficient as she showed Lily into Patterson's office, not bothering to offer her coffee. This time, she wasn't greeted with a smile. Patterson's dour expression clearly telegraphed the subject of their meeting. She'd never been fired before, but now that she'd accepted her fate, she felt almost calm.

"Miss Gallagher, please sit down."

Lily shook her head. "I can stand. Just say what you have to say."

Patterson nodded his head. "All right. We're no longer in need of your services. After that photo in the paper, I don't think anyone in the media is going to take you seriously. And I get the feeling that your relationship with Brian Quinn isn't working to my benefit. I've called your boss and told him that he can keep half the retainer. He asked me to tell you he expects you in the office first thing tomorrow morning."

"Mr. Patterson, I know I haven't been very effective, but DeLay Scoville can help you with your public relations work. We have an outstanding staff and highly qualified and effective personnel. If you just give us a chance, I can recommend another consultant who could be here in the morning, ready to jump right in."

"There's no need. I've already contacted a firm in New York."

At that, Lily knew it wouldn't pay to argue any longer. Patterson had already made up his mind. And now that it was over, all she could think about was getting out. "Fine. I'll just clear out my things. But I would like to tell Marie that she still has a job here."

"She does," Patterson said.

"Thank you." Lily turned and walked out, then took the stairs down to her office. She paused on the landing between the two floors and drew a deep breath. "That wasn't so bad," she murmured. "I suppose everyone has to be fired at least once in their lives." But now that she was out of one job, she couldn't help but wonder if she'd be out of a second one soon. And if she found herself out of a second, then that opened up a whole new world of possibilities.

Her mind wandered to Brian Quinn, but Lily shook her head, banishing the image of him from her mind. Yes, he'd asked her to marry him, but Lily couldn't believe he was serious. The Quinn family curse was a ridiculous reason for marriage and one she had no intention of considering.

"SHE'S GONE."

Brian sat down on the arm of the sofa in Sean and Liam's apartment. Though he could say the words, he still couldn't believe them. It had all happened so quickly that he hadn't had time to react. After the free-for-all at the ground-breaking ceremony, he'd been hesitant to call Lily. He'd wanted to give her time to recover—and time to forget what he'd said. And now she'd disappeared.

Hell, he hadn't meant to bring up marriage. He'd just been so frustrated that it had come out. Yes, it had sounded a little crazy, but he'd lived with this damned curse hanging over his head for such a long time, it seemed like the logical next step.

"Did you leave her a message?" Liam asked.

His little brother was stretched out on the sofa, a bag of potato chips resting on his stomach, a beer in his hand. Sean, sprawled in a tattered easy chair, rested his stockinged feet on the coffee table. Though Liam was usually never far from Ellie, tonight she was in Hartford, attending a seminar, leaving all three brothers single again.

"She's not out," Brian explained, "she's gone. Left. Disappeared."

"I'd probably take off, too," Liam said. He pointed to the copy of the *Herald* that Sean had tossed on the coffee table. "That's not a very flattering photo. I mean, what kind of lens was that guy using. Whatever it was, it makes her ass look bigger than Fenway."

"Shut up," Brian said. "She has a really nice ass."

"I'm just saying that the depth of field is bad. The guy was probably using an auto-focus camera and with that kind of lighting, the shadows are going to enhance the curvature and you won't get—"

"Liam, shut yer gob," Sean shouted, throwing a pillow at his brother's head. "Can't you see our boy is upset?" He turned to Brian. "What are you going to do?"

"I thought I had this all figured out," Brian murmured. "I decided to drop the story. Not exactly drop it. I gave my files to this rookie reporter at the station. I wanted to tell Lily, so I called her at work and the receptionist told me that she no longer worked for Patterson. Then I called her hotel and she'd already checked out."

"So consider yourself lucky," Sean said. "It looks like you avoided the Quinn family curse."

"I don't think I did," Brian muttered. "I'm in love with her." He groaned softly, then pinched his eyes shut. "You know, I thought this curse was just a load of crap, but it isn't. When it hits you, it hits hard, like a truck. I haven't known her for a month, but I know one thing—I want her in my life."

"Then go get her," Liam said.

"I don't know where she is. I know she lives in Chicago, but I couldn't get her phone number from information and I don't remember the name of the place where she works. And Patterson sure as hell isn't going to give it to me." He glanced over at Sean. "Maybe you could help?"

Sean shook his head. "Are you crazy? Break it off now, clean and simple."

"You're refusing to help me?" Brian asked. He strung together a long list of curse words. "All right, I'll pay you."

"If you marry her, I'm the only one left," Sean said. "I don't want to be the only one left."

"So find yourself a woman," Liam suggested.

"No way," Sean muttered. "Are you even sure that it's the curse? You never saved her life, did you?"

Brian frowned. "No. Not in a big way. But in lots of small ways that probably added up. I saved her from that dolt at the fund-raiser and she nearly walked right into the street in front of a car and she almost fell down the stairs. And there was a bike in the park and the flying fish. It all adds up."

"Are you trying to convince us or convince yourself?" Sean asked.

"He's right," Liam said. "Compared to what I did for Ellie, that doesn't seem like much."

Brian pushed to his feet and began to pace back and forth between the door and the sofa. "I didn't set out to fall in love with her, but I'm sure that's how I feel. I told her that, but I don't think she believes me. How the hell am I supposed to convince her when I'm not even sure how to explain it myself?"

"You just feel it in your gut," Liam said. "That's how it was with Ellie."

"Lily thinks it's all about the sex."

"Good sex?" Liam asked.

"Great," Brian murmured. "Better than great. All I have to do is touch her and boom, we're ripping each other's clothes off. I have no self-control around her. I think about her all day long and can't sleep because I can't put her out of my head. But it's not just about the sex. There's more to it than that."

Sean groaned and threw his arm over his eyes. "Stop, please." Suddenly, he cursed and then jumped to his feet. "Come on, Li. If I have to listen to any more of this whining I'm going to punch him."

"Where are we going?"

"To find Brian's woman. I know a maid over at the Eliot. Maybe she can get us an address and phone number off the hotel registration."

"Good," Brian said, walking with them to the door. He rubbed his hands together. "All right. Now I have a plan. Right now, I've got to go to the station. I have a report that airs on tonight's news. Meet me at the pub afterward and you can tell me what you found."

His brothers nodded and walked out the front door, leaving Brian alone in the apartment. He sighed softly as he began to pace again. This would have to work. He'd get Lily's address and go to Chicago and convince her that they belonged together.

There was still the matter of where to live. He had a job here. And the *Globe* was still a possibility. But then, there were great television stations in Chicago and a world-class newspaper.

Brian stopped. "What am I doing? I don't even know how she feels about me. Love first and then logistics."

As he stepped outside and walked to his car, he had reason to hope. He loved Lily Gallagher and if he loved her, then he could make it work the same way his brothers had made it work. A *Mighty Quinn* didn't give up.

LILY HAD PACKED up her things and checked out of the Eliot Hotel in a matter of minutes. She hadn't bothered to fold her clothes carefully, knowing she wouldn't be wearing them to work any time soon. She'd just stuffed them in her bags and forced the zippers closed.

Travel to the airport had been easy—a cab to the water shuttle and the water shuttle to Logan. Though she hadn't called ahead for a ticket, Lily found a seat on the 7:30 p.m. flight to Chicago, checked her luggage, and sought out the closest bar to her gate. That had been nearly eight hours ago and in that time, she'd switched from margaritas to club soda and back to margaritas again.

Her flight had first been delayed by weather. They'd boarded an hour late and then been hustled back off the plane when a mechanical problem was discovered. The airline staff had reassured the fifty or so passengers that the flight would leave that night, but wouldn't commit to a time.

"Can I get you anything else?" the bartender asked.

Lily pushed the nearly empty bowl of peanuts toward him. "Could I have more free snacks?"

He smiled and nodded, then drew a club soda for her and placed it in front of her. "On the house."

"I guess it's time to switch back." Lily sighed. "How much longer can they keep us here?"

"As long as they want," he said, sliding a fresh bowl of peanuts down the bar. "Hey, it's good for our business." He wandered off to tend to another customer and Lily glanced up at the television. The sound was down, but she tried to follow along with a popular cop show. When the commercials came on, she glanced away. But something brought her gaze back to the screen.

Lily's breath caught in her throat as she watched a late news cut-in. Brian Quinn stood against a city backdrop. He spoke, then pointed over his shoulder at some large tanks, his expression filled with concern. Lily couldn't look away, captivated by the handsome face that she'd grown to love, the dark hair and golden-green eyes. Her gaze fell to his mouth and a flood of sensation raced through her as she remembered what he'd done to her with that mouth.

And then he was gone, a car commercial replacing his image. She drew a ragged breath and an ache settled in around her heart. Lily glanced at her watch. It was nearly ten and the news came on at eleven. She probably wouldn't be here to see his report.

Lily fought a flood of emotion. She didn't want to believe that this was the last time she'd ever see him. Until this moment, it hadn't hit her that she was walking away from a man who claimed he loved her, a man who was convinced he was supposed to marry her.

"This isn't the way it's supposed to work," Lily muttered. They were supposed to meet and date and get to know each other. And then, they were supposed to fall in love and talk about marriage. And then, maybe they'd get engaged and walk down the aisle.

With Brian, it had all been turned upside down. Nothing had happened in the right order and to top it off, what *had* happened had occurred in the course of a month. People didn't fall in love in a month! And they didn't fall in love with a one-night stand.

But as Lily tried to think about Brian Quinn in a calm, rational manner, memories of their time together kept creeping back in. He'd never once lied to her. He'd never hurt her or insulted her or cheated on her. He'd respected her work and yet challenged her ideas without judging her. And when he touched her, he took her to places she'd never been before.

Lily groaned softly and put her head down on the bar. Why was she leaving this man? In her whole history with men, she'd never once met one who possessed all those qualities. And now that she had, she was walking away simply because she couldn't make it fit her preconceived notion of what love was supposed to be.

But it wasn't about her brain, it was about her heart. When she stripped away all the logic and common sense, Lily knew she felt something for Brian Quinn, something soul-deep and sure. Maybe it was love. She closed her eyes and when she opened them again, Lily knew exactly what she needed to do.

She grabbed her purse and dropped some money on the bar. "Thanks," she called to the bartender.

"Is your flight leaving?"

"Nope. I decided not to go."

Lily hurried back to the ticket counter and told them that she'd be staying in Boston. Since her luggage had already been checked, she didn't want to wait around for it to be taken off the plane, so she arranged to pick it up the next morning. She wasn't even sure where she'd spend the night, but right now that didn't make a difference.

The water shuttle back across the harbor seemed to take twice as long as it had coming and when they finally reached the dock, Lily jumped off and grabbed the first cab she could find. But as she sat down in the back seat, she realized she wasn't sure where she ought to meet him. It was almost eleven. By the time she reached the station, he might be gone already. She'd never been to his apartment, but she had been to the pub. She'd start there.

"Quinn's Pub," she said. She gave him the directions she remembered from her first cab ride there, then settled back into the seat. A tiny smile curled the corners of her mouth and suddenly Lily knew exactly what she was doing. There were no doubts, no fears. She'd go to Brian and find out exactly how he felt. And if she couldn't see it in his eyes, then she hadn't lost anything in trying.

Resolved, Lily nervously counted the seconds as the cab made the quick trip from Rowes Wharf to South Boston. As they came closer to Quinn's Pub, Lily's pulse began to quicken. And when the cab stopped in front of the pub, she had a moment of indecision. But she paid the cabbie anyway and stepped out.

The pub was busy, but not crowded. When she walked inside, she scanned the place for Brian. She saw him at the end of the bar and her heart skipped a beat. And then she realized it wasn't Brian at all, but his twin brother, Sean. She slowly approached him and when she caught his eye, smiled. He nudged the guy sitting next to him and he looked up as well.

Lily swallowed hard. "Hi."

"Hello," Sean said.

"You don't know me. I'm Lily Gallagher. I'm looking for Brian."

"She's the one," Sean muttered.

The other man grinned and held out his hand. "I'm

Brian's brother, Liam. The youngest. It's nice to meet you, Lily. Brian's told us so much about you."

"He has?"

"Well, he might have mentioned you a few times," Liam said. "And we saw your photo in the *Herald*. I'm a photographer. I probably would have tried for a more attractive angle."

Lily groaned inwardly, a blush warming her cheeks. "I was hoping to find Brian here," she said.

"Oh, he'll be here," Liam said.

"He's supposed to meet us," Sean added.

She nodded, uneasy beneath their intense scrutiny. Though she'd felt completely at ease with Brendan, she got the distinct feeling that Sean didn't like her. And that Liam found her presence at the pub to be highly amusing. He couldn't seem to stop grinning.

"You want to play some darts while you're waiting?" Liam asked.

Lily shrugged. "I don't think I've ever played darts. I probably wouldn't be any good. I'm just going to go find a place to—"

"Come on," Liam teased. He grabbed her arm and drew her along with him. "You're a girl. We'll let you win a few. It'll be fun."

They strolled back past the pool table to an open area with two dartboards on the wall. Sean retrieved the darts and handed her four of them with little yellow plastic feathers on the end. Lily thanked him, then laughed softly. "I can't believe how much you two look like each other."

Though it was easy to see they were twins, there were more obvious differences. Where Brian was confident and outgoing, Sean seemed to be almost painfully shy. He stood just far enough away so that he wasn't forced to join in the conversation and Lily couldn't help but wonder what was behind that dark and brooding facade.

Liam moved to stand behind her, then positioned the dart in her hand. "Hold it like this," he said. "And then just smoothly draw your arm back and loft the dart forward." He showed her the movement a few times, then stepped away. "Give it a try."

Lily focused on the target, trying to repeat what Liam had shown her. But when she threw the dart, it spun end over end, hit the wall a few feet from the dartboard and fell to the floor.

"That was...not good," Liam teased. "Try again."

She threw three more darts and they all ended up bouncing off the wall and landing on the floor."

"Maybe pool is your game," Liam said.

"You don't have to entertain me," Lily said. "I can just get a drink and sit down."

"Sean, go get Lily a Guinness." Liam pointed to a booth. "Why don't we sit there."

Lily took a spot across the table from Brian's brother. She smiled. "If you want to play darts, you can."

"Nah, I'll sit here with you. If you decide to leave and I'm not here to stop you, Brian will kick my ass." Sean set a glass of Guinness in front of each of them, then wandered back to the bar. "He thought you left town," Liam said.

"I was on my way, but there are a few things left to be said and I just wanted to say them before I went home."

Liam nodded. "He really likes you, so if you're going to dump him, it would probably be best for you to just go."

"I didn't come here to hurt him. We just need to talk."

Liam looked over her shoulder to the door. "Well, you won't have to wait any longer."

Lily twisted around to see Brian walking through the door. She quickly stood and brushed her hair back from her eyes, then stuck her nervous hands in the back pockets of her jeans. He didn't notice her at first as he made a quick search of the bar. But then Lily took a few steps forward.

His eyes met hers in the same way they had that night at the fund-raiser, holding her attention so she couldn't look away. They slowly approached each other and met in the middle of the bar. Though Lily knew that most of the patrons were watching them, she didn't care.

She wasn't sure what to say, but then Brian took care of that. He cupped her face in his hands and kissed her, his mouth devouring hers like a man taking a drink after days in the desert. Lily's heart raced and she could barely breathe, but she knew that she'd made the right decision. He did love her. It was all there in his kiss, every ounce of emotion he felt for her.

When Brian finally drew back, the patrons of the bar burst into wild applause, shouting and whistling. Brian pulled her into a hug and chuckled. "We have an audience."

"I hope this doesn't end up on the front page of the *Herald* tomorrow."

"It won't, I promise." He grabbed her hand and drew her along with him to the door. The crowd at the bar groaned, but Brian just waved at them as they stepped out into the humid July night. When they reached the street, he pulled her into his arms and kissed her again, this time lingering over her mouth.

"You came back," he murmured, nuzzling his face into the curve of her neck.

"I never left," Lily said. "I was at the airport and then I decided I couldn't go."

"Why not?"

"I had to talk to you. I had to find out for sure."

"What?"

"The other night, in the elevator, you told me you were falling in love with me. And then, that day in the news truck, you said you wanted to marry me. If I walked away from that, I knew I'd always wonder."

Brian smiled down at her. "I didn't say I wanted to marry you," he murmured, running his thumb along her lower lip.

Lily stepped back, stunned. "But you—"

"I said that I'd *have* to marry you."

"Oh," she murmured, her heart sinking. She'd misunderstood completely. This wasn't happily-ever-after. Mortified, she turned and began to walk away, not sure what she ought to do.

"I do love you, Lily," Brian said.

She stopped, then slowly turned back to him. "You do?"

He nodded. "And I am going to ask you to marry me...just as soon as I'm sure you're going to say yes."

"You are?"

He shrugged. "I know we haven't had a conventional relationship. But I promise, if you'll let me, I'll make you happy for the rest of your life. We may not do everything the right way or in the right order, but I think that's what makes things so good between us. We never know what's going to happen next."

"I don't have a job," Lily said. "I'm going to resign my job in Chicago."

"Hell, I'm thinking about quitting mine, too."

"You are?"

Brian nodded. "I think I have to start doing something that doesn't involve my face. The *Globe* has a position open for a staff writer. It's a big cut in salary, but I know I can make it work, Lily. If you stay here with me, I can make it work. Can you live in Boston? Because, if you can't, then we'll go to Chicago."

Lily smiled, her heart warming. He loved her and he wanted her in his life...forever. She wanted to jump up and down and shout, but instead, she stepped back into his embrace. "I'll go wherever you go. And if we stay in Boston, then we'll make a good life here."

Brian grabbed her around the waist and spun her around. "I tried so hard to avoid falling victim to the Quinn family curse. But it's not a curse at all," Brian murmured. "It's like having your best wish come true."

Lily hugged him hard, then noticed a crowd watching them from the windows of the pub. She smiled at them and gave them a thumbs-up. With that, they all began to cheer again, the noise audible through the windows.

Brian turned around and waved at them, then grabbed Lily's hand and pulled her along the sidewalk to his car. "Come on, let's get out of here."

"Where are we going?" she asked.

"I'm taking you home—to bed. It's about time we started doing things the normal way."

Lily stopped short, yanking him back into an embrace. "And I was just thinking how much I liked things the way they were. You know, it's a warm night. And I've never made love outdoors. You think there might be a spot somewhere in Boston where we could give that a try?"

Brian growled and kissed her hard. Then he smiled down at her. "I could get used to having you around all the time."

Epilogue

BRIAN GRABBED the coffeepot and filled his mug, then dumped a healthy measure of Rice Krispies into a bowl. A can of concentrated orange juice thawed on the counter, but he couldn't wait. He grabbed a spoon and tried unsuccessfully to pry it out of the can and into a pitcher. "Lily! We're going to be late. If you want a ride, you're going to have to be ready in five minutes." He poured milk onto his cereal and took a hasty bite.

A few seconds later, Lily rushed into the kitchen, buttoning the front of her blouse, her jacket tucked beneath her arm. "I know, I know. I have to look just right. I have a big client meeting this morning." She straightened and smoothed her hands over her skirt. "We have to work out some kind of schedule in the bathroom," she said. "There has to be a way for us to co-exist in there."

Brian looked up from his bowl of cereal, his gaze taking in her disheveled appearance. They'd lived together for nearly two months and he still enjoyed the little moments like this, when it hit him that Lily wasn't going anywhere, that she was with him for the rest of his life. "We could always get a new apartment, someplace with a bigger bathroom."

"Or two bathrooms," Lily suggested.

She tucked her blouse into her skirt, then slipped

into her jacket. The suit was a taupe-colored fabric that looked like linen, a conservative style paired with a clingy silk blouse. Brian thought she looked especially beautiful that morning, but then she always looked beautiful.

"Are you almost ready?" he asked.

"You're the one who kept me in bed too long," she said, taking a bite of his cereal. "If you want me on time, then we're going to have to wake up earlier."

"So what's the meeting about?" he asked, watching her draw her hair back at her nape.

"It's my first real paying client. Do you think I should wear my hair up or down?"

"Up," Brian said.

"Really?" She frowned. "I was thinking down. I want to appear businesslike but approachable."

"Is the client male or female?" Brian asked.

"Female," she said.

"Then down. Definitely down."

"And if my client was a male?"

"Up. In one of those prissy little knots."

Lily shook her head and laughed. "I don't think I trust your advice."

Brian grabbed her around the waist and kissed her neck, leaving milk on her skin. "You'd look beautiful if you teased your hair and wore it with a big bow on top of your head. Trust me."

"We're going to be late," she warned. "You're not a big shot at the *Globe.* like you were at the TV station. They won't tolerate tardiness."

"How could they fire their newest feature writer?" Brian asked.

Lily gasped as she drew back. "Feature writer?"

"I've been assigned my first investigative piece. I'm no longer going to be just 'staff writer.' Pretty good for two months on the job."

He'd decided to take the job at the *Globe* the day after Lily decided to stay in Boston. He and Lily had enjoyed a few weeks of freedom before he started at the paper and in that time, she'd made plans to start her own public relations consulting firm. They found her office space in one of Rafe's buildings and she gradually began to make contacts in and around Boston.

Though they were living on a fraction of what they'd both previously earned, Brian didn't care. They had each other and that was enough. There would be plenty of time to make money later. For now, making love was more important.

"Congratulations, darling," Lily threw her arms around his neck and kissed him, a tempting kiss that made him think of things other than work. Brian returned her kiss, picking her up and setting her on the edge of the kitchen table, then sliding his hands along her thighs.

"Thank you, sweetheart," he murmured.

"What are you doing?" Lily asked as his hands moved up to the buttons on her blouse.

"Are you sure you don't want to dance? We have a little time before we have to leave for work. And we do have something to celebrate. Richard Patterson is going to prison for a few years. Did you see the article in the paper? It was very romantic."

"Romantic?"

"He was the man who brought us together. As I was reading it, I felt this urge to propose."

Lily groaned, then slapped his hands away. "If you

keep teasing me like this, I'm not going to say yes. Come on, I have a meeting. Let's go."

Brian brushed his hand over his jacket pocket where he'd tucked the little velvet box, waiting for the right moment to present her with the ring. For now, he'd save it. "All right. Let's go. I'm pitching my first story at the editorial meeting this morning."

"What's your story about?" she asked, reaching around him to grab the bowl of cereal. She fed him a spoonful, then took one for herself.

"The Boston Fund," he said. "It's a charity that—"

"I know it's a charity," Lily said, the spoon freezing halfway to her mouth. "It's run by Dorothy Elton Fellner."

"Right. I've learned that dollar for dollar she spends more on her balls and receptions than she does on the less fortunate of Boston. She's using her charity to fund her social life. It's just a big scam and some of the most prominent people in this city have been duped."

Lily groaned. "No. Are you sure?"

"I've talked to three different sources and they all tell the same story. Amy, Brendan's wife, says it's a well-known fact among the rest of the charities in town. And Fellner uses the nonprofit status to avoid taxes." He kissed her again. "Now, who is your new client?"

A tiny smile touched her lips. "My new client is Dorothy Elton Fellner," she said. "She wants me to plan her next event and do some publicity for the charity."

Brian stared into the eyes of the woman he loved, then chuckled softly. "I can't believe this has happened to us again."

"I can't either. What are we going to do?"

"I have another idea I could pitch," Brian suggested. "And I suppose I don't really need her business," Lily countered.

He'd never imagined that he and Lily would be faced with another professional conflict. But now that they'd made a life together, Brian didn't really care about the story. He'd found a woman to love and she was worth any compromise. "Take the job," Brian said.

"I'll forget the story."

Lily shook her head. "No, it will make a great story. You do it."

"We could flip for it," Brian said.

Lily wrapped her arms around his neck. "I'll give you this one, Brian Quinn. But you're going to owe me."

Brian bent close and kissed her, lingering over her mouth for a long time before he stepped back. The Quinn family curse had struck yet again but as he looked into Lily's beautiful face, Brian realized that although a curse had brought them together, it was love that would keep them together.

With Lily in his life, he'd become a *Mighty Quinn*. Not the kind of Quinn who could slay a dragon or bring down an ogre. But the kind of Quinn who could love a woman every day for the rest of his life. And though his story might not be told in years to come, he knew it would be the greatest adventure of his life.

Another *Mighty Quinn* had found love and in finding love, had discovered his heart.

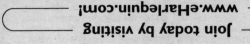

eHARLEQUIN.com

The eHarlequin.com online community is the place to share opinions, thoughts and feelings!

- **Joining the community is easy, fun and FREE!**
- **Connect with other romance fans** on our message boards.
- **Meet your favorite authors** without leaving home!
- **Share opinions** on books, movies, celebrities...and more!

Here's what our members say:

"I love the friendly and helpful atmosphere filled with support and humor."
—Texanna (eHarlequin.com member)

"Is this the place for me, or what? There is nothing I love more than 'talking' books, especially with fellow readers who are reading the same ones I am."
—Jo Ann (eHarlequin.com member)

Join today by visiting
www.eHarlequin.com!

If you enjoyed what you just read, then we've got an offer you can't resist!

Take 2 bestselling love stories FREE!
Plus get a FREE surprise gift!

Clip this page and mail it to Harlequin Reader Service®

IN U.S.A.	IN CANADA
3010 Walden Ave.	P.O. Box 609
P.O. Box 1867	Fort Erie, Ontario
Buffalo, N.Y. 14240-1867	L2A 5X3

YES! Please send me 2 free Harlequin Temptation® novels and my free surprise gift. After receiving them, if I don't wish to receive anymore, I can return the shipping statement marked cancel. If I don't cancel, I will receive 4 brand-new novels each month, before they're available in stores. In the U.S.A., bill me at the bargain price of $3.57 plus 25¢ shipping and handling per book and applicable sales tax, if any*. In Canada, bill me at the bargain price of $4.24 plus 25¢ shipping and handling per book and applicable taxes**. That's the complete price and a savings of 10% off the cover prices—what a great deal! I understand that accepting the 2 free books and gift places me under no obligation ever to buy any books. I can always return a shipment and cancel at any time. Even if I never buy another book from Harlequin, the 2 free books and gift are mine to keep forever.

142 HDN DNT5
342 HDN DNT6

Name	(PLEASE PRINT)	
Address		Apt.#
City	State/Prov.	Zip/Postal Code